# RESET BUTTON

## Paul Root

dizzyemupublishing.com

DIZZY EMU PUBLISHING

1714 N McCadden Place, Hollywood, Los Angeles 90028

dizzyemupublishing.com

**RESET BUTTON**
Paul Root

First published in the United States
in 2021 by Dizzy Emu Publishing

dizzyemupublishing.com

# RESET BUTTON

Paul Root

RESET BUTTON


Screenplay
Paul Root


LOGLINE
Thirty something "ne'er do well" Cameron is told his dear
Grandmother, Peggy, has cancer, and not long to live.
Unable to cope, Cameron hits rock bottom, until Peggy
tells him if he completes a To-Do list, he stands to
inherit a secret family fortune. After a chance meeting
with the steel willed and wild Laura, Cameron is swept
around the world to complete the list, and finally
have a life worth living...but can he accept it?

WGA #1985275 (01/25/2024)

RESET BUTTON

PORTLAND, OREGON - MODERN DAY - MARCH - REAL WORLD SETTING

INT. MAGGIE'S DINER - EARLY AFTERNOON

CAMERON THOMAS, 30s, white, soulful eyes, well groomed,
expressive but unassuming, sits in an orange vinyl diner
booth.

Across from him is his Grandmother PEGGY SHERMAN (June Squibb
Type), 80s, wearing an orange polyester dress, and apron,
with bright blue name tag. A waitress, ALEXA, 20s, wearing
the same, tops off their coffee, and leaves.

                         PEGGY
              Thanks, darlin'.

A silent moment before Peggy digs in her purse, and removes
a pack of Newport cigarettes. She taps it against the faux
wood laminate table top, shaking Cameron's keys on the
formica.

Peggy slides a cig out and puts it to her lips.

                         CAMERON
              You gotta be fucking kidding me...

                         PEGGY
              Ruined my first cigarette in forty
              years!

Peggy throws the cig into her purse.

                         CAMERON
              How long?

                         PEGGY
              Forty years! I just told you!

Cameron stares her down.

                         PEGGY (CONT'D)
              A year.

                         CAMERON
              What's the treatment plan?

                         PEGGY
              'Treatment plan?!' HA! Honey, at
              this point, I'm not worth the price
              of a bullet.

                         CAMERON
              You should be home, Peggy.

                    PEGGY
          You don't tell me *shoulds* and
          *should'nts*, Cameron. I'll haunt you.

                    CAMERON
          Haunt me...right. I'm sure it'll be
          a real "Revenge of the Fallen."

He "air quotes," this. Peggy looks at him blankly.

                    CAMERON (CONT'D)
          You got that movie for me for
          Christmas, or my birthday fourteen
          times.  Remember that specifically.
          14. I don't know why it had to be
          THAT movie. It's not important. You'll
          be buried with it.

                    PEGGY
          I bought a whole display at Wal-Mart,
          for the Boys and Girls club thanks
          very much! Still have about, I don't
          know, a hundred of em. Boys and girls
          club doesn't want 'em anymore. What
          am I supposed to do with them?!

                    CAMERON
          Not buy them in the first place?

Peggy scowls. Cameron is somber. He takes a breath and glances
at her

                    CAMERON (CONT'D)
          What can I do here, Peggy?

Cameron stares into her with desperation. Tears are forming.

                    PEGGY
          Don't cry. It does me no good, and
          you look hideous when you do it.

He comes back around with a chuckle.

                    PEGGY (CONT'D)
          You working tonight?

                    CAMERON
          I took it off. In case you needed
          me.

                    PEGGY
          Bullshit. You just don't wann-

                    CAMERON
          Peggy, if, IF something happened and
          I weren't around I would...I.
               (beat)
          I don't know. I would never forgive
          myself. OK?

                    PEGGY
          OK, Honey... So, what are you up to
          then?

                    CAMERON
          Seeing a friend.

Cameron hesitates. Knowing what's coming, he snags his keys
from the table.

                    PEGGY
          Michelle?!

                    CAMERON
          Peggy, please not ri...

                    PEGGY
          I swear you never learn. One of these
          days I'm gonna write a list of ACTUAL
          THINGS for you to do!!

                    CAMERON
          Looking forward to that. I gotta go.

                    PEGGY
          I don't know wha...

                    CAMERON
          Peggy not right now...please?

                    PEGGY
          Fine then. We still on for my
          birthday?

                    CAMERON
          Yes. Blazer Game. Saturday.

                    PEGGY
          My favorite boys with my favorite
          boy!

Peggy smiles and opens her arms. He smiles and hugs her tight.
He fights the tears this time.

                    CAMERON
          Love you.

                         PEGGY
               I love you too. Now go on before I
               slap some sense into you.

Peggy wears a look of concern as he walks out, and slides
out a fresh Newport.

EXT.  MICHELLE'S APARTMENT - LATER - LATE AFTERNOON

Cameron's car, a basic import sedan, pulls up outside of
Michelle's trendy looking apartment building in Portland's
Pearl District.

INT.  MICHELLE'S APARTMENT - CONTINUOUS

MICHELLE, 30s, very pretty, dark eyes, cunning, lies on a
black leather couch, wearing a short black trench coat and
thigh highs. Cameron walks in and stops dead in his tracks.

                         MICHELLE
               Hard day?

                         CAMERON
               That's not the only thing...

Michelle grins at him slyly. Cameron throws himself on top
of her and they kiss passionately.

INT.  MICHELLE'S BEDROOM - LATER

Loud moans over the darkness as Cameron and Michelle are
finishing. Their heads hit the pillows as they breathe heavily
for a few seconds.

                         MICHELLE
               Did you miss me?
                    (beat)
               You fucked me like you missed me.

Michelle leans over and kisses his neck and chin.

                         CAMERON
               I missed you...

Michelle smiles, turns to her nightstand, and pulls out a
baggy of cocaine. Michelle pours a few small piles on the
nightstand. She grabs a pre-rolled hundred.

                         CAMERON (CONT'D)
               A hundred?

                         MICHELLE
               Feels cool.

Cameron shrugs as Michelle leans to snort. Michelle does the standard nose pinching/sniffing after.

                         MICHELLE (CONT'D)
          You good?

                         CAMERON
          Yeah yeah I'm good.
              (beat)
          Just the Peggy stuff.

                         MICHELLE
          Is it a big deal; can it wait?

                         CAMERON
          Nah.
              (beat)
          Not a big deal.

Michelle kisses his cheek, snorts another bump, then hands the bill to him. He hesitates, then leans over her, and snorts the bump. Michelle laughs as he reacts. He snorts another then excitedly kisses her neck and shoulders.

INT. MICHELLE'S BEDROOM - NIGHT

Cameron and Michelle are asleep in her bed.

Suddenly! -- SFX - KLUNK CLINK KLUNK - !!!

It's the front door opening. They spring up.

                         MATT  (O.S.)
          Babe?
              (inaudible)
              (beat)
          Michelle?

Michelle looks at her phone, grabs a robe, then runs to the door.

                         MICHELLE
              (whisper yelling)
          Stay here! Don't move!

Michelle leaves, closing the door behind her. Cameron quickly puts on shorts and a tee from his bag. He glances at the clock. 11:11pm.

INT. MICHELLE'S APARTMENT - CONTINUOUS

Cameron walks into the living room, sees Michelle, and then MATTHEW, any ethnicity, preppy and tidy, early 20's, holding a bowl of chicken noodle soup, and wearing lobster hot mitts. They're all frozen for a moment before....

> CAMERON
> Who the fuck are you?!

> MATTHEW
> I should ask you the same!

> MICHELLE
> Matthew LEAVE! Cameron just...uuummm

As Michelle stammers, Matthew storms toward him, still holding the soup. Michelle steps between them.

> MICHELLE (CONT'D)
> MATTHEW, GET OUT!

> CAMERON
> What the fuck is going on?!

> MATTHEW
> I'm her frickin' boyfriend, guy!
> Who're you?!

Cameron's gaze darts to Michelle. He stares at her for a moment, then turns and walks to the bedroom.

> MICHELLE
> Cameron, wait!

> MATTHEW
> "Cameron wait?!"  What a-

> MICHELLE
> MATTHEW GET OUT!

INT. MICHELLE'S BEDROOM - CONTINUOUS

Cameron grabs his stuff and snags the bag of coke from the nightstand on the way out.

> MATTHEW  (O.S.)
> I'm not going anywhere!

INT. MICHELLE'S APARTMENT - CONTINUOUS

Cameron walks into the living area with Michelle and Matthew still squaring off.

> CAMERON
> I'm fuckin' outta here. Listen, Max
> or Matt or Mark...

> MATTHEW
> Matthew!

                    CAMERON
          Matthew, sorry...I suggest you do
          the same.

Cameron is already walking toward the door.

                    MICHELLE
          Cameron, just, wait...listen to me!

Michelle follows him out the door as Matthew sits on the
couch still holding the soup.

EXT. MICHELLE'S APARTMENT - CONTINUOUS

A basic apartment exit and courtyard in Portland's Pearl
District.

                    MICHELLE
          Cameron just listen to me for a
          second! Please...

He doesn't break stride. Michelle catches up to him.

                    MICHELLE (CONT'D)
          He's not my boyfriend!

                    CAMERON
          Why did he show up unannounced at
          eleven PM with a house key, soup,
          AND FUCKING LOBSTER MITTS, MICHELLE?!

                    MICHELLE
          We've dated...just off and on. I was
          gonna see him tonight, but you said
          you wanted to come by so I told him
          I was super sick. He just showed up!

                    CAMERON
          Fuck. He's a fuckin' sweetheart...
               (beat)
          I shouldn't have texted you. You
          cheated on me, and now you do this
          to, basically, I don't know, a teenage
          Henry fuckin' Winkler?!

                    MICHELLE
          Cameron please...

Without hesitating Cameron piles into his car, and drives
off.

INT.  CAMERON'S APARTMENT - BEDROOM - LATER

Cameron lies in his sparsely decorated bedroom. A bedside
alarm clock transitions from 1:54 to 1:55am.

He skims blankly through the dating app HINGE, Elliot Smith
dramatically croons in the background. He swipes a few times,
and then LAURA RODRIGUEZ, Latina, steely, intense eyes, soft
but strong, honest, 30s. He stops and skims her profile.

                         CAMERON
               Hiiiiiii.

A text comes through from Michelle.

                         CAMERON (CONT'D)
               Shiiiiiit.

He pulls open a nightstand drawer and grabs the stolen baggy
of coke. He makes a line and rolls a bill from his wallet.
He snorts it hard.

                         CAMERON (CONT'D)
               OK I'm ready.

He opens the message.

MICHELLE TXT: Can we talk?

A moment, then text bubbles appear on the screen

MICHELLE TXT: When you said something happened with Peggy I
had to see you.

More bubbles...

MICHELLE TXT: Please text when you see this tomorrow.

Bubbles

MICHELLE TXT: Its ok about the coke

He goes to settings, blocks her number, and tosses the phone
aside.

                         CAMERON (CONT'D)
               I need a drink.

INT. SPIRIT OF 77 BAR - LATER

Cameron, shutting and locking the front doors, pockets his
keys, and saunters in to Spirit of '77 (Portland Trail Blazers
fan bar with 50 TVs, seating for 100+, and a bank of pop-a-
shot machines.

He's fully dressed for the day with a Blazers cap on. He
pours himself a pint glass of Jim Beam on the rocks, and
plops on a barstool. He channel surfs, and stops on
"Kindergarten Cop." Schwarzennegger is on a gurney.

                    LITTLE BOY ON TV
              Mr. Kimball, are you alright?

Cameron snickers, chugs half the glass, then begins to cry.

INT. SPIRIT OF 77 BAR - MOMENTS LATER

Cameron climbs into one of the pop-a-shot machines, dunking
balls through the cylinder, eventually breaking it, which he
celebrates with a thunderous roar, then throws the rim across
the empty bar as a crescendo.

He snorts cocaine off the bar top

He sweeps and mops the floor

He attempts a one man keg stand in various ways/methods

He watches some of the AM SportsCenter/First Take

He dusts various areas

He hits a vape pen

He poops in a urinal

He passes out on the door mat at the front entrance cleaning
the glass.

INT. SPIRIT OF 77 BAR - LATER

The sun shines on Cameron's unconscious body through the
front doors. One swings in, hitting Cameron's leg. He doesn't
move. TYLER, 20s/30s, any ethnicity, hipster, nerdy handsome,
walks in holding two coffees.

                         TYLER
              Cam...CAM!!

Tyler shoves Cameron with his toe a bit, then kicks him.
Cameron turns over and groans as the sun hits his face.

                         CAMERON
              Morrrrrrrninnnng

                         TYLER
              First two times kinda funny, not
              funny anymore.

INT. SPIRIT OF 77 BAR - LATER

Tyler sits, and sets down a cup of coffee. Cameron sits next
to him, Windex in hand.

                    CAMERON
          Thanks, man.

He takes a big swig, and pulls a twenty out of his pocket.

                    CAMERON (CONT'D)
          Consider it a service fee.

Tyler looks around at the swept and mopped bar.

                    TYLER
          The bar looks amazing.

Tyler slides the twenty back to Cameron. Cameron cheers'
with his coffee cup.

                    TYLER (CONT'D)
          What happened there?

Tyler points at the broken pop-a-shot machine rim on the
floor.

                    CAMERON
          I needed to fix it anyway.

                    TYLE
          Yeahhhh. So...
               (beat)
          What the fuck is up, man?

                    CAMERON
          Peggy has cancer.

                    TYLER
          Fuck. I...how bad?

                    CAMERON
          Stage four bone in her hip. And
          Lymphoma. And Glaucoma. She's
          just...being her about it?

Tyler pours two shots, and slides one to Cameron.

                    TYLER
          Little hair of the dog, on me.

                    CAMERON
          To a true original. Maybe the last
          one.

They cheers, and shoot.

                    TYLER
          I'm gonna hit the bathroom and open
          up.

Tyler rounds the bar.

                         TYLER (CONT'D)
               Oh shit. Hey, Trent didn't come in
               to cover your yesterday so you still
               gotta finish all the bills and stuff.

                         CAMERON
               Fucker! Um, yeah, ok I got it. Thanks.

Tyler walks into the men's room. A moment passes...

                         TYLER  (O.S.)
               WHAT THE HELL, MAN?!

                         CAMERON
               WHAT?!

Tyler comes back out fuming.

                         CAMERON (CONT'D)
               What's wrong?!

Tyler storms over, yanks the twenty from Cameron's hand, and
points to the bathroom. Cameron looks confused, and walks
over.

                         CAMERON  (O.S.) (CONT'D)
               Yeah, that's my shit.

INT. SPIRIT OF 77 BAR - OFFICE - LATER

Cameron sits at his desk staring at a stack of envelopes in
a tray marked "BILLS." The one at top is from a beer
distributor. Cameron snags it and looks it over.

                         CAMERON
               Due YESTERDAY. Shit. Thanks, Trent.

He goes through some other bills before shoving them away in
aggravation. He drops his head into his hands and sighs. He
pulls his cocaine baggy from his pocket. Hardly a bump left.

                         CAMERON (CONT'D)
               Fuuucccckkkk!

Cameron digs to an unsaved number buried in his text history.

Text: "Party favors?"

EXT. SPIRIT OF 77 BAR - LATER

Cameron meets a DEALER outside the bar across the street.

INT. SPIRIT OF 77 BAR - MOMENTS LATER

Cameron opens the baggy making two separate lines. He snorts
them quickly, and turns on a bluetooth speaker. The Protomen,
cover of "I Still Believe," fills the air. Cameron closes
his eyes and begins to dance in his chair.

He grabs the stacked bills and a calculator.

(Cameron slams through in a fast motion time lapse with money
math equations flying around the room.)

INT. SPIRIT OF 77 BAR - LATER

Cameron makes rounds talking with bar patrons, having a good
time. Cameron approaches the bar, and slams a shot as A GLASS
BREAKS and then...

                    LAURA  (O.S.)
          Fucking pervert! Grab my ass again,
          I fucking dare you!

Cameron spins around. Lo and behold it's Laura from Hinge at
1am, pushing JOE, 20's, tall, who dropped and broke his pint
glass.  Laura throws a drink in his face. Joe stumbles
backward and over a stool landing on his ass.

Cameron lets out a bellowing laugh. He and Laura exchange a
glance and grin, still not quite recognizing the other.

Joe, angry and embarrassed, directs his attention to Cameron.

                    JOE
          Think that's funny, asshole?

Joe charges Cameron.

                    CAMERON
          Oh boy.

He dodges. Joe turns and punches him in the back. Cameron
turns and Joe punches him in the shoulder. Cameron growls,
tackles him, and the punches fly.

After taking a couple shots, Joe wiggles away, and out the
door. Cameron takes chase, and gets just outside before he
pukes, and collapses.

INT. SPIRIT OF 77 BAR - MOMENTS LATER

Laura stands dumbstruck with her friends witnessing this.
Cameron sits up in the window.

                    LAURA
          This is too good.

Laura pulls her phone out and takes a photo, leaving the
flash on. Cameron is startled and turns toward her. He stares
for a moment.

                    CAMERON
          I know you?

He falls to the pavement again. Laura takes another pic.

INT. SPIRIT OF 77 BAR - NEXT DAY

Cameron walks in, and removes his sunglasses. He has a black
eye courtesy of Joe. Tyler, who is mopping, stops.

                    TYLER
          I've been trying to cover for you,
          man. I know you're going through
          some shit...but...the getting wasted
          and shitting in urinals, and after
          last night you're late today...I don-

                    CAMERON
          I know. It's ok.

At this moment we hear owner, TRENT GALLOWAY.

                    TRENT   (O.S.)
          Cameron. Office. Now.

INT. SPIRIT OF 77 - OFFICE - MOMENTS LATER

Cameron walks in, Trent, white, all Gucci clothes, know it
all, power trip, 40s is already seated, arms crossed. They
stare at each other. After a moment...

                    TRENT
          So you got into a fight with this
          "Joe" last night; and apparently you
          pissed yourself?!

                    CAMERON
          I didn't piss myself. I puked on
          myself. Dude was a creep, Trent.

                    TRENT
          We'll get back to that. You didn't
          send out checks to pay beer bills,
          Cam. There are a bunch of games,
          including BLAZER GAMES. At my BLAZERS
          BAR, and now I'm kinda fucked. Not
          to mention I could end up getting
          sued by this guy!

                    CAMERON
          Trent, I've let my recreational shit
          get out of control, I know, but I
          have **killed it** here for five years.
          I've missed weddings, birthdays,
          even funerals, man. And regardless,
          you didn't show up like you said you
          would.


                    TRENT
          You could have done it any day the
          whole last week. I also see your bar
          tab is over twelve hundred dollars?!


                    CAMERON
          You know I'll pay it.


                    TRENT
          You already have, buddy.


                    CAMERON
          Trent, my quasi girlfriend's boyfriend
          walked in on us the other night...I
          just found out Peggy has cancer.

Trent tosses Cameron's baggy of cocaine onto the desk.
Cameron knows he's fucked for sure. Trent picks up an envelope
from the desk, and shoves it into Cameron's face.

                    TRENT
          Last check minus the tab. Sorry,
          Cam. Especially about Peggy, but I
          gott-

Cameron snatches it violently, and BAM! He punches Trent in
the face.

INT. SPIRIT OF 77 BAR - CONTINUOUS

Cameron and Trent come tumbling out the door punching,
kicking, etc. Both get to their feet. Cameron goes into a
rage. He swings, misses. Trent punches him in the chest.
Cameron screams like a yet to be discovered animal.

                    TRENT            TYLER
          The fuck?!         The fuck?!

Trent bolts toward a nearby door. Cameron intercepts him in
a bull rush and tags him with his shoulder sending Trent
flying through a large window, and onto the outside pavement.
Cameron stumbles and steadies.

He looks out, and sees Trent bleeding on the sidewalk,
surrounded by broken glass.

                    TRENT
          Fuuuuccccckkkkk!!

                    TYLER  (O.S.)
          Fuck!

                    CAMERON
          Fuck....

INT.  PORTLAND JAIL - MORNING

Cameron walks to the wall mounted phone with a GUARD (any
ethnicity, 40s-50s) in the Multnomah County Jail.

                    GUARD
          One call. ONE.

Cameron lifts the wall mounted receiver, and puts it to his
ear. He only knows one number from memory. He hesitates, and
dials.

                    CAMERON
          Grandma! You'll never guess where I
          am...
               (beat)
          I call you "Grandma," all the time.
               (beat)
          Yes I do!

EXT. JAIL - LATER

Cameron walks with Peggy into the parking lot from the jail
entrance. Cameron turns on his phone; notifications flood
in. One is a Hinge message from Laura. He opens it.

MESSGAGE - OH MY GOD. You're the drunk manager from Spirit
of 77! (Crying laughing emoji) Sorry not sorry.

Cameron rolls his eyes, and shoves the phone in his pocket.

                    PEGGY
          I'm missing my morning shift at the
          shelter AND Blazers basketball because
          I had to bail YOU out of JAIL on MY
          BIRTHDAY. You owe me eleven dollars
          for the Lyft I took here too.

                    CAMERON
          We can still go to the game, Peg-

                    PEGGY
          Ohhhh no. You get to sit in this. Do
          you think I acted like such a shit
          bag when I lost your Grandfather? Or
          your Mother?

Cameron is fuming, but it's beginning to process. Peggy will
be gone soon, no way around it.  His body slumps as serotonin
flows in, and their Lyft arrives.

                    PEGGY (CONT'D)
          I wanna show you something.

They pile into the car.

INT.  CASA DE PEGGY - LATER

Cameron sits in Peggy's living room. It's decorated in middle
high-end decor from a franchise type furniture store in the
late 80's, lots of gloss black and glass. Peggy walks in and
sets down a mug of tea, and a dusty photo album, and sits.

                    CAMERON
          I don't need to see myself naked at
          the piano right now.

Peggy, wipes the blue leather cover with a towel, and opens
it. Cameron peeks over at the page. His eyes widen.

                    CAMERON (CONT'D)
          That's Jack Nicholson!

A picture of a Young Peggy with Jack. They toast drinks toward
the camera.

                    PEGGY
          1976. I met him at a party in Los
          Angeles after a Blazers Lakers game.
          So charming. I woulda slept with him
          if it weren't for your Grandfather.
          Come to think of it, Earl probably
          would've forgiven me...

                    CAMERON
          Stop! Stop...
              (beat)
          You're serious?

                    PEGGY
          I forgave him for Woodstock.

                    CAMERON
          Woodstock?! What did you d...No...I
          don't wanna know.

Peggy flips the page. It's one large photo of she and Earl,
marked with the name/location of a beach in Ibiza.

                    PEGGY
          That was my favorite trip. Ibiza.
              (MORE)

                    PEGGY (CONT'D)
          Most gorgeous place on earth. 1981.
          We jumped off that cliff in the
          background there.

He takes it in before Peggy flips again.

                    PEGGY (CONT'D)
          Berlin wall in eigthy-nine. West
          German side.

We see a photo of 40 something Peggy doing her best "Rosie
the Riveter," pose as the wall is being destroyed.

Peggy flips the page again. A photo of Peggy and friends,
RUTH, YVONNE, and LYNNE. They stand just to the side of a
racetrack in Turin, Italy with a group of strapping Italian
lads, one holding a trophy.

                    PEGGY (CONT'D)
          I was 19. A few years before I met
          your Grandpa. I went to Turin with
          the girls and we had a helluva time!
          I met a man ther...

                    CAMERON
          No details.

                    PEGGY
          Right. Well. You really should drive
          a Ferrari sometime. Such great fun!

Another photo of the four women standing amongst a few
Ferraris with some drivers and other tourists. Cameron's
mouth is agape. Peggy turns the page again marching in a
PRIDE parade in the 1990s.

                    CAMERON
          This is unreal. Why haven't I seen
          this? Why haven't you TALKED about
          this?!

                    PEGGY
          I don't remember you asking. You
          could use some of that living. Take
          advantage of the post COVID world.

                    CAMERON
          I've lived, OK? You have NO idea.

                    PEGGY
          Sniffing cocaine off some girls hind
          end at, I don't know, "Big Corey's"
          house party isn't living life.
                    (MORE)

                    PEGGY (CONT'D)
          We got your passport years ago, and
          you haven't been **anywhere**. Heavens
          sakes, you didn't even leave for
          college!

                    CAMERON
          Peggy, I can't travel, or adventure,
          or go on a vision quest, or whatever
          the hell. I have no money...or job.

                    PEGGY
          There's plenty you can do!

                    CAMERON
          I know the this place inside and
          out. We've been all over it. And
          regardless...I. AM. BROKE. I have
          four-hundred thirty-three dollars.
          Trent's probably gonna sue me.  I'll
          be lucky if I don't move back in
          with you.

A silence.

                    PEGGY
          I can't believe I love you this much.

Cameron is mildly offended. There's a long beat here.

                    PEGGY (CONT'D)
          What if I gave you a sort of
          allowance?
               (beat)
          I pay all your bills, and give you
          say...five-thousand a month?

Cameron laughs, but Peggy looks back completely stone faced.
Cameron sits closer to her, feeling some legitimate concern.

                    CAMERON
          Do I need to call Doctor Choudry?

                    PEGGY
          Cameron, your Grandfather and I
          invested VERY well. We have never
          wanted for anything.

Cameron studies her, absorbing this information.

                    PEGGY (CONT'D)
          Shoot, we lived off of Earl's Jeopardy
          winnings for almost three years.

                    CAMERON
Grandpa was on Jeopardy?!

                    PEGGY
Grandpa WON Jeopardy. Four days.
Back in seventy-nine.

                    CAMERON
Wh...w...why did we clip coupons?
Why did we shop at Value Village?!
Why DIDN'T we have cable? Why did I
EVER eat bologna?!

                    PEGGY
Mostly to save money. The bologna I
just like.

                    CAMERON
I always thought we were just
"scraping by."
        (beat)
Why do you still work at a diner?!
Retire. You're 85 years old.

                    PEGGY
86.

                    CAMERON
86. Happy Birthday. Sorry...Fuck...

                    PEGGY
You've spent the last couple years
content to float through life wasting
time with Michelle. You need a kick
in the ass, and this is it. I'll
open the trust up for you early.
With conditions...

                    CAMERON
Done.

                    PEGGY
Not so fast. The "to-do list," I
threatened you with?

                    CAMERON
No...

                    PEGGY
Yes. I'll have five-thousand dollars
released to you every month for a
year.
                    (MORE)

                    PEGGY (CONT'D)
          You can spend it, you can save it,
          put it up your god damn nose if you
          want to; you can do whatever your
          little heart desires with it. It's
          your money.

                    CAMERON
          What's the catch?

                    PEGGY
          You don't finish the list, you don't
          get the rest of the money.

                    CAMERON
          Which is how much exactly?

                    PEGGY
          Rude. Gift horse here.

Peggy extends her hand. Cameron, impressed, looks at it, and
eventually shakes it.

                    PEGGY (CONT'D)
          Go get a pen and paper. I want to
          write this thing. I'm on a roll.

                    CAMERON
          I can do it on my phone...

                    PEGGY  (O.S.)
          OOOOOOHHHH NO. Were getting this
          notorized. We're gonna see a lawyer
          too. I don't trust you.

Cameron is stupefied.

                    PEGGY (CONT'D)
          Cancer. Time is of the essence. The
          pen and paper...GO!

Cameron walks toward a hallway.

INT. CASA DE PEGGY - LATER

Cameron and Peggy sit at the table, now with a couple of
empty glasses and plates. A litany of papers with all sorts
of shit scribbled and scratched over them are strewn about.

A single clean and neat list is in front of them. Peggy
finishes writing in an item.

                    CAMERON
          You want me to go to Florida?

                         PEGGY
               Ruth and the girls haven't seen you
               since you were nine, and...

                         CAMERON
               Not my fondest memory, Peggy.

                         PEGGY
               I'll have you know that karaoke
               performance comes up in conversation
               all the time.

                         CAMERON
               That lip sync is an all-time cringe
               moment. It needs to be erased from
               existence. Not reliving that for a
               weekend. Thanks, but no thanks.

                         PEGGY
               There's a small fortune riding on
               this.

                         CAMERON
               I'll go visit your old lady friends
               and have tea. Fine.

Peggy writes this down "MEET YOUR FATHER" as the FIRST item.
Cameron crumples the paper, springs up, and goes to toss it,
but, Peggy intercepts.

Peggy motions for Cameron to sit. He does. Peggy writes on a
separate paper: Doug Bennett. 6600 ne 33rd st Phoenix, AZ.
Cameron springs up from the couch again.

                         CAMERON (CONT'D)
               Peggy what the FUCK?!

                         PEGGY
               Cameron SIT DOWN!

He does.

                         PEGGY (CONT'D)
               I want you to listen, cause I'm saying
               this once.

Cameron sits still and quiet. The Dad thing was a bomb.

                         PEGGY (CONT'D)
               You don't have to live a fancy life,
               but you better damn well live a good
               one. You need to do this.

He takes a deep breath and stares into her.

INT. OFFICES OF BALDWIN, HARVIN, & LOCKETTE - MORNING

We see....

THE LIST

Scribbled at top of the wrinkled page MEET DOUG

1.  Leave the country (belgium, ireland, india)

2.  Take an acting class (fail)

3.  Take martial arts classes (miami)

4.  Drive a Ferrari (vegas)

5.  Put it all on black (vegas)

6.  Help the animals (vegas)

7.  Go skydiving (miami)

8.  Go Surfing (italy)

9.  Learn a second language (pieces)

10. Visit Ruth, Yvonne, and Lynne (miami)

11. Shoot a gun (austin)

12. Perform Stand Up (fail NYC)

13. Swim with sharks (fail)

Cameron, a happy pug GEOFF in his lap, and Peggy sit at the desk of SUSAN KRIEG 50s (Octavia Spencer Type), glasses, very professional, upbeat/perky personality. The offices are very posh. Modern and clean.

                    SUSAN
          Essentially, if this list isn't
          complete at the event of your death
          all assets will be divided between
          charities to be determined at a later
          date.  Correct?

                    PEGGY
          Couldn't have said it better myself,
          dear.

                    SUSAN
          Basically requirements in terms of
          inheritance. Standard thing, but
          what a fun way to to it!
                    (MORE)

                    SUSAN (CONT'D)
          Shouldn't take more than a few days
          to write up.

Peggy takes her card from a holder on the desk.

                    PEGGY
          Susan, I just couldn't appreciate it
          more.

                    SUSAN
          It's no problem. I love paperwork.
          Why I got into estate law. I'm one
          of "those."

                    PEGGY
          You're just a doll! Let me get you a
          coffee this week! I wanna hear this
          whole story.

                    SUSAN
          Would love to!

                    CAMERON
          WOW! SUPES FUNS! Can you two do this
          later?

          PEGGY                        SUSAN
Cameron, shut your shit        Mind your manners!
can! Lord...                   What is wrong with you?!

                    PEGGY
          Susan, it was truly lovely to meet
          you.

                    SUSAN
          And you, Peggy! I'll send over the
          paperwork this week.

Cameron sets down Geoff, who waddles to a corner dog bed.

                    CAMERON
          Sorry...um, for that.

                    SUSAN
          I hope so...Bye, Cameron.

                    CAMERON
          Bye. Later, Geoff.

Geoff breathe/grunts as he rolls around in his bed.

INT. PEGGY'S CAR - MOMENTS LATER

Cameron is driving them to Peggy's house in her Honda Accord.

                    PEGGY
          So, when ya headin' to Phoenix?

                    CAMERON
          Six-twenty tomorrow.

                    PEGGY
          If it's the morning I'm not drivin'
          ya.

                    CAMERON
          Appreciate that. Yes, in the morning.
          Doesn't actually land until after
          two with layovers.

                    PEGGY
          Take your passport. And get the most
          comfortable shoes you can find. Here.

Peggy shoves an envelope in his coat pocket. He glances at
his beat dark blue and grey leather Nike blazers.

                    CAMERON
          Because?

                    PEGGY
          The passport, because you'll need
          it. The shoes, because your feet
          will thank you. If there's anything
          not right about your shoes in Europe
          you'll be miserable.

                    CAMERON
          I'm not going from Phoenix to Europe,
          Peggy.

                    PEGGY
          The card in that envelope is attached
          to an account with $5,000 in it, and
          gets another $5,000 a month starting
          next month. Pin is 6969. I figure
          you'd remember that.

                    CAMERON
          Am I that basic?

                    PEGGY
          Absolutely.

                    CAMERON
          I love you too.

Cameron leans over and hugs her.

INT. CAMERON'S APARTMENT - BEDROOM - NEXT MORNING

The clock reads 4:33a. Cameron looks like hammered shit, but
is dressed, awake, and finishing packing with a ball cap on.
He pulls his passport from his nightstand. He flips through
it. No stamps, no nothing. He tosses it in the bag.

EXT.  BOEING 737 - LATER

Cameron sits in a window seat staring out, headphones in.

EXT.  DOUG'S STREET - PHOENIX LATER - DAY

Cameron's rental car, a late model sedan, stops a house away
from his destination.

INT. CAMERON'S RENTAL CAR - CONTINUOUS

Cameron double checks the address. He pulls a vape pen from
his bag, hits it, slips it back.

EXT.  DOUG BENNETT'S HOUSE - MOMENTS LATER

Cameron slumps up the steps, and leers at the door to his
Father's home. He hesitantly knocks. The door opens to reveal
DOUG BENNETT 50s/60s (WOODY HARRELSON TYPE), aged well, kind
eyes, carries himself gracefully, in his robe and boxers.

Cameron lifts his phone, puts on a shit eating grin, and
grabs Doug around the shoulder, pulling him in close for a
selfie.

                    DOUG
          What the hell?!

                    CAMERON
          Say cheese. CHEEEEESE!

Cameron snaps the picture of he and the unkempt Doug, who
recoils with the flash.

                    DOUG
          Wait a second!

Cameron looks at the phone, and walks away satisfied with
the photo. Doug follows after him for a second then...

                    DOUG (CONT'D)
          CAMERON!

Cameron, just reaching the front of his rental, stops in his
tracks. Cameron can't move. He's in total shock. He's never
met this man. Doug approaches, closing and tying his robe.

                    DOUG (CONT'D)
          Thanks for stopping.

                    CAMERON
          I want to keep going, my body
          just...won't go.

                    DOUG
          Just come in. Cameron, please.

Doug walks toward the house, Cameron hesitantly follows.

INT. DOUG BENNETT'S HOUSE - CONTINUOUS

Doug closes the door behind Cameron as he looks around the
house. There are framed pictures of him, he and Peggy/his
mom, sports team photos, school photos, you name it, amongst
the sparsely furnished and decorated home.

                    CAMERON
          The fuck is all this?!

                    DOUG
          Peggy sent 'em. Here, she gave me a
          heads up you'd be comin'.

Doug paws through the mail on a nearby table, and brings him
a same day envelope from Peggy. Cameron takes it, and reads
quietly. He drops like a sack of potatoes onto the couch. He
looks around at the photos again, and laughs.

                    CAMERON
          What do you tell people when they
          come over and see all this?

                    DOUG
          That I have a son in Portland.

                    CAMERON
          My perspective: You have pictures of
          a fucking child STRANGER all over
          your house. Pretty fucking weird,
          man. What am I even supposed to talk
          to you about? "You from around here,
          buddy?!"

                    DOUG
          Nope. Texas.

                    CAMERON
          That's EXACTLY the problem! You
          already know where I'm from!

Silence

                    CAMERON (CONT'D)
          Do you have a beer? I need a beer.

INT.  DOUG BENNETT'S HOUSE - KITCHEN - LATER

Cameron sits at a table with a can in front of him. Doug
opens a kitchen cabinet, and shuffles some things.

                    CAMERON
          Just you here?

                    DOUG
          Since Daisy passed, yeah.

                    CAMERON
          That a woman you had captive?

                    DOUG
          My dog.

Doug points to a picture of a cute yellow lab on the wall.
He turns around with a large shoebox, and drops it on the
table.

                    DOUG (CONT'D)
          And stop with the comments.

Cameron rifles through the box with his fingertips.

                    CAMERON
          So, you and Peggy talk...

                    DOUG
          Not so much any more. That was the
          first letter in about seven years.

                    CAMERON
          Funny. I haven't gotten one in thirty-
          three.

                    DOUG
          When I promised your Mothe--

                    CAMERON
          Don't. Don't do that, man.
               (beat)
          I want to leave, but I'm stoned, and
          I'm trapped here and just...don't.

                    DOUG
          OK.
               (beat)
          How about brunch? On me.

                         CAMERON
          Make it a drink.

                          DOUG
          You can drink at brunch if you want.

                         CAMERON
          Perfect. I'll get a Lyft. You change.

Doug looks down at his robe and nods. Cameron retrieves his
phone from his pocket.

EXT. PHOENIX BAR - MORNING - LATER

The Lyft stops to let them out in a fairly packed parking
lot. As Cameron gets out of the Lyft, the VALET at the front
of the building makes some sort of exchange with a man getting
his car. It's a drug deal.

                         CAMERON
          Go ahead inside. I gotta make a call.

Cameron dials the Hall & Oates emergency call line
(719.266.2837) as Doug flashes a thumbs up and heads in.
Cameron chooses 'Private Eyes,' from the menu, waits for a
moment, and jogs to the valet podium.

                    CAMERON (CONT'D)
          Heeeeyyyyy buddy...

INT.  PHOENIX BAR - LATER

Cameron and Doug sit across from each other at a high top
table in the packed neighborhood sports bar. People chatter,
hoot and holler at sports sporadically.

A SERVER (any age/gender/ethnicity) comes over and drops a
fresh pitcher.

                         SERVER
          There you go gents.

                          DOUG
          Thanks very much.

Doug pours them each a pint. Cameron notices a woman across
the restaurant. They exchange a glance. Cameron chugs half
of his beer.

                         CAMERON
          Be right back.

Cameron walks away in a hurry.

INT. PHOENIX BAR - BATHROOM - MOMENTS LATER

Cameron is in the bathroom stall. He quickly lines up some cocaine on the toilet tank, and snorts it.

INT. PHOENIX BAR - MOMENTS LATER

As Cameron walks out of the bathroom, rubbing his nose, he sees VERONICA 20s/30s, a tall attractive brunette, at a stand up table with a German Short-Haired Pointer. He slides up next to her.

                         CAMERON
          Gorgeous.
               (soft beat)
          The pointer. What's his name?

                         VERONICA
          This is, Thor.

He pets the happy dog, THOR.

                         CAMERON
          Thor! I love it. Pointers. Great
          dogs. So eager, and handsome. Remind
          me of me.

They laugh. Her more kind of grossed out.

                         VERONICA
          Right.

                         CAMERON
          I would love to come back later
          tonight and buy you a drink.

                         VERONICA
          Up to you...

She gestures to an enormous man, WALTER 30s, 6'5"+, jacked, tatted, at the bar. Veronica waves, Walter waves back.

                         CAMERON
          Boyfriend?

                         VERONICA
          Not exactly.

                         CAMERON
          In that case...ten?

                         VERONICA
          Sure...

Cameron heads back over to Doug. He's high as shit, and
feeling really good about himself. He pounds the last half
of his beer.

                         DOUG
               What was that about?

                         CAMERON
               Plans for later. Very excited!

Cameron fills his glass from the pitcher. Doug looks at his
face/eyes/nose and can tell he's wasted.

                         DOUG
               I see. You happen to know the man-
               beast that's walking over to her?

                         CAMERON
               What?

                         DOUG
               He's staring at you, and I don't
               think it's because you're pretty.

Walter stomps their direction.

                         CAMERON
               Shit...

Close up Walter is even more terrifying. The man is massive,
eyes are like black pools, arms like anacondas.

                         WALTER
               You hitting on my wife?

Walter gestures toward Veronica.

                         CAMERON
               I didn't mean anything by it, man.

                         WALTER
               You did though. You're trying to
               meet her back here at ten.

                         DOUG
               He's was joking. He stays with me.
               I apologize. Let me pay your tab.

                         WALTER
               Need your senior discount boyfriend
               to save your skinny ass?

Everyone in the bar is looking now.

                    CAMERON
          OOOOOOK, you can fuck off.

Walter cocks his fist back. Cameron ducks. Doug gets punched
square in the face and hits the deck. (Cameron is not
flamboyant here. This is matter of fact in delivery)

                    CAMERON (CONT'D)
          This man just punched my boyfriend!
          You could have killed my very old
          boyfriend! You all heard him!

Doug looks at Cameron as if he is crazy. Cameron bears down
with his eyes, Doug then nods.

                    CAMERON (CONT'D)
          No one follow us out or I'm calling
          the cops!

Cameron and Doug stumble outside.

INT. DOUG BENNETT'S HOUSE - LATER

Cameron walks into the living room with an ice pack. Doug
puts it on his chin.

                    DOUG
          Do me a favor. Next time you're on
          coke and hit on a woman that's spoken
          for, leave me out of it.

                    CAMERON
          What are you talkin' about?

                    DOUG
          I know the signs. I've had my fun.
          Didn't even get to finish my beer.

Doug pulls out a joint. They both laugh. Doug lights it,
takes a puff, and hands it to Cameron.

                    DOUG (CONT'D)
          So....You haven't heard my end. You
          wanna?

                    CAMERON
          Were here.

                    DOUG
          Guess I'll take that...
               (beat)
          Your Mom and I met over spring break
          senior in college.
                    (MORE)

                    DOUG (CONT'D)
          (beat)
     I was so smitten with her. Like,
     immediately. Your Mom was an
     incredible fuckin' woman. She had a
     lot of her Mom in her I think. I
     didn't give a shit that we were broke
     doing long distance trying to finish
     college. I couldn't let her go.
          (beat)
     Fast forward a couple years, and we
     had to face reality, and a couple
     months after that day I get a letter,
     no return address. She's pregnant.
          (soft beat)
     I called fifty times, sent a dozen
     letters to the last address I had.
     Eventually I showed up. She moved.

                    CAMERON
     Why?

                    DOUG
     I wish I knew. One day outta the
     blue, years later, I get a letter
     from Peggy that your Mom has cancer.

                    DOU
     Peggy said I could write. I could
     see you anytime. I could call anytime.
          (beat)
     We get a weekend picked out, I'm
     finally ready. I ask Peggy to keep
     it secret. I lose my job. I freak
     out, I cancel.
          (beat)
     I fall into some shit, deep. Long
     time. In the pictures, before I knew
     it...I was looking at a man.
          (beat)
     Peggy always said I could stop sending
     payments, that it would be bet-

                    CAMERON
     Time out. What the fuck are you
     talking about "payments?"

                    DOUG
     I sent seven hundred a month to Peggy
     for 20 years.

                    CAMERON
     Bullshit.

Cameron looks furious.

                    DOUG
          Nope. No matter what, I always did
          that. Ask her yourself.

Cameron's expression softens.

                    CAMERON
          Planning on it.

                    DOUG
          You do that.
               (beat)
          I'm gonna hit it.

Doug gets up and heads for his bedroom.

                    DOUG (CONT'D)
          Goodnight.

INT. DOUG BENNETT'S HOUSE - KITCHEN - MORNING

Cameron pours coffee into a thermos and seals the top. He
notices a mail organizer on the wall, red/pink envelopes
peeking out. He rifles through them.

One an overdue mortgage bill for nearly nine-thousand dollars,
car loan four months overdue etc. He hears Doug shuffling
around upstairs, and quickly reorganizes the papers.

EXT. DOUG BENNETT'S HOUSE - MOMENTS LATER

Cameron and Doug stand on his front step. Cameron has his
bags piled next to him.

                    CAMERON
          Can I borrow this?

He holds up the thermos.

                    DOUG
          Consider it a gift.
               (beat)
          I was a...I was thinkin' last night
          and why I didn't ever ah...reach
          out.
               (beat)
          Really, I just was scared.
               (beat)
          And I th--

                    CAMERON
          I was scared too, man.

Doug hugs him intensely. Cameron hugs him back. After a second

                    CAMERON (CONT'D)
          Ok. Ok.

They separate.


                    DOUG
          So, was this a one shot deal?


                    CAMERON
          Left my info on the counter.


                    DOUG
          Then I'll be in touch.
               (beat)
          Where to now?


                    CAMERON
          Driving the rental up the coast.
          It's "picturesque," according to
          Peggy. Then flying to Miami.


                    DOUG
          She's right. But, if you have a couple
          days, you should head to Austin.
          The food, the music, everything.
          That's home. Austin in Texas.

Cameron walks to the car and tosses his bags in the trunk.


                    CAMERON
          When you say "Austin," people assume
          Texas I'm pretty sure. Get a dog or
          something, Doug.


                    DOUG
          I just might. Have a safe trip.

Doug waves. Cameron reciprocates, piles in, drives off.

INT. CAMERON'S RENTAL CAR - MOMENTS LATER

Cameron calls Peggy on bluetooth. It goes to voicemail.


                    CAMERON
          Hey, Pegggg. Would have been nice to
          know that Doug was sending SEVERAL
          HUNDRED DOLLARS OF CHILD SUPPORT
          EVERY FUCKING MONTH FOR MOST OF MY
          LIFE AND YOU TWO CHIT CHATTED ALL
          THE FUCKIN TIME. WOULD HAVE BEEN
          NICE TO HAVE SOME COOL SHIT OR
          SOMETHING SINCE YOU WERE A SECRET
          BEZOS BECAUSE OF CHILD SUPPORT AND
          GAME SHOWS.

He hangs up. A few moments later a text comes through from
Peggy. He taps the screen and the car robot voice reads it
aloud

CAR ROBOT VOICE: Don't read this while driving. That money
was used to support you, as was intended. Doug knew we didn't
need but insisted on sending. You have money now. Buy all
the "cool shit" you want.

                        CAMERON (CONT'D)
              STOP SOUNDING SO FUCKING LOGICAL,
              ROBOT! FUUUCK!

Cameron pulls the car over on the freeway. He types AUSTIN,
TX into the GPS. 13 hours. He hits the "GO," button.   ETA
9:22 pm.

INT. CAMERON'S RENTAL CAR - LATER

Cameron is rocking out to "DARE," by Stan Bush. He sees a
NIKE SWOOSH on the side of the freeway. He contemplates,
then pulls off.

EXT. NIKE STORE PARKING LOT - LATER

Cameron walks to his rental car with bags in hand, and an
Air Jordan 11 Cool Grey (2 tone grey w white and patent
leather SKU CT8012-005) on his feet and "DARE" by Stan Bush
playing over.

EXT.  FREEWAY - LATER

Cameron's rental car is stopped in front of a sign that says
"Welcome to Austin." He stands in front of it, extends his
arms, snaps a photo, and gets back in the car.

INT.  FAIRMONT HOTEL - AUSTIN - NIGHT

Cameron walks through the hotel lobby with his bags. As he
approaches the desk the RECEPTIONIST (any age/ethnicity)
greets him.

                        RECEPTIONIST
              Welcome to the Fairmont. How can I
              help you, sir?

                        CAMERON
              Anything available?

                        RECEPTIONIST
              Absolutely, sir. What are you looking
              for?

                        CAMERON
              What's good?

                    RECEPTIONIST
          I have a king bed deluxe room with
          breakfast included for three-eighty-
          eight per night.

                    CAMERON
          Sold. Tonight and tomorrow night.
          Please.

Cameron sets down a card and his ID. The receptionist begins
plugging in info.

                    RECEPTIONIST
          Perfect I'll go ahead and book that
          for you now, sir. What brings you to
          Austin?

                    CAMERON
          Uuuummm...A whim honestly.

                    RECEPTIONIST
          Sounds great! Welcome. Here's your
          room keycard. Anything else I can do
          for you, Mr. Thomas?

                    CAMERON
          Actually, yeah, can you recommend a
          place for dinner?

INT.  THE ROOSEVELT ROOM BAR - LATER - NIGHT

Cameron sits at the bar top of the fancy/vibey Austin spot
chatting with the bartender ZACH, soft spoken, big beard,
30s/40s..

                    CAMERON
          Another, please. And pour one for
          yourself on me.

                    ZACH
          Don't have to tell me twice. Where
          you bartend?

Zach pours two. They cheers and down them.

                    CAMERON
          Portland. You can always tell.

Zach smiles, and pours two more.

                    ZACH
          Yup. What brings you to Austin?

                    CAMERON
          I just wanted to get away for a few
          days.

                    ZACH
          Good choice. Austin is a cool town.
          I'm from Miami.

                    CAMERON
          I'm heading there in a couple days.
          Small world.

                    ZACH
          Never ceases to amaze me. I'll be
          back, give you some spots to check
          out. None in South Beach.

They cheers and shoot again. Zach heads to the other end of
the bar to help customers (any age, ethnicity). Cameron sits
in silence a moment before heading to the bathroom.

INT. THE ROOSEVELT ROOM BAR BATHROOM - MOMENTS LATER

"Weight" by Freddie Gibbs plays over as Cameron moves in
slow motion, almost silkily, to the bathroom stall door. He
opens it, and begins to line up the coke from the baggy onto
the toilet tank in high stylized flair.

Cameron throws his head back after railing the line. He grins
cheekily.

INT. THE ROOSEVELT ROOM BAR - MOMENTS LATER

Cameron walks out of the bathroom and there in the middle of
a birthday party is Laura. He stops dead. He pulls his phone
out and checks Hinge. They're still matched. Her current
city is Austin.

                    CAMERON
              No way...

Laura is laughing at something as she scans the bar when
suddenly her gaze locks onto him.

                    LAURA
              No way...

LAURA'S FRIEND turns to Laura.

                    LAURA'S FRIEND
              What?

                    LAURA
          That's the manager from Spirit of
          '77!

                    LAURA'S FRIEND
          The fight and puke guy from Portland?!
          No wayyyyyyyy. Where?!

Laura points at him, then gets up and walks toward him.

                    LAURA'S FRIEND (CONT'D)
          Laura, no! Very scary!

Cameron stumbles back towards the bathroom, accidentally
into the ladies. Laura follows.

INT.  THE ROOSEVELT ROOM LADIES ROOM - CONTINUOUS

Cameron crashes into one of the stalls, hitting the floor.

                    LAURA
          What the fuck are you doing here?! I
          will mace your face!

                    CAMERON
          I'm high! I'm very high! Fuck I'm
          high!

                    LAURA
          Come again? Are you high?!

Cameron frantically rips the bag of coke from his pocket,
shakes it into the toilet and flushes it. Laura stands at
the stall door.

                    LAURA (CONT'D)
          Good call. You couldn't do that in
          the men's room though?

                    CAMERON
          All bathrooms are for all people!

                    LAURA
          Nothing is for anyone over 30 that
          wears those shoes.
               (beat)
          Actually, I can't decide if you're
          pulling those off. How old are you?

                    CAMERON
          Why are you here? What are you doing
          here?!

                    LAURA
          Not important. Why are YOU here?

                    CAMERON
          It's a small world...It never ceases
          to amaze me...hahahhaah
               (MORE)

                    CAMERON (CONT'D)
          (beat)
     I need to get home. And water.

                    LAURA
     Shit...Come on. Let's get you a cab.

Laura helps him up, and walks out. Cameron follows for a
step, and stops in front of the mirror. He's a walking Nick
Nolte mugshot. He sighs heavily and takes a picture of himself
with his phone as his hands shake, and he slinks out.

EXT. THE ROOSEVELT ROOM - MOMENTS LATER

Cameron and Laura stand at the bar entrance as a Lyft arrives.
He's OUT OF IT.

                    LAURA
          Don't make me regret this, but I put
          my number in your phone...this is
          just too weird.

                    CAMERON
          Thanks for not macing my face. And
          cab.

                    LAURA
          Another time I'm sure. Sleep on your
          stomach.

Laura walks away as Cameron flops into the car.

INT. THE FAIRMONT HOTEL - CAMERONS ROOM - MORNING

Cameron is passed out, face down, on his posh hotel room
bed. His phone vibrates next to his head. He wakes up, and
groggily answers.

                    CAMERON
          Yeahhhhhh?

                    PEGGY (V.O.)
          Hey, Mister! Just checkin' on ya.
          You said you'd be here by ten today
          and it's after eleven.

                    CAMERON
          I'm in aaahhhhh Austin?

                    PEGGY  (V.O.)
          TEXAS?! You sure? Ya don't sound too
          sure.

                    CAMERON
          I'm sure. Long night.

                    PEGGY  (V.O.)
          I'm gonna let the girls know you're
          going to Miami from there instead of
          here then.

Cameron hears what he is sure is Peggy taking a drag from a
cigarette?

                    CAMERON
          OK. Are you smoking?

                    PEGGY  (V.O.)
          Of course not. Did it go ok with
          your Dad?

                    CAMERON
          Weirdly ahh yeah. Peggy, did any of
          this money, for this, thing, did it
          come from Doug?

                    PEGGY  (V.O.)
          No. I gotta get back to work. I love
          you bunches!

                    CAMERON
          Love you too...

The line clicks off. Peggy hung up. He hangs up and sees he
has a text from "Laura Lifesaver."

Laura - "alive?"

Cameron calls her.

                    LAURA (V.O.)
          You defied the odds. Congrats.

                    CAMERON
          Still touch and go at this stage.
          Have you eaten yet?

INT.  AUSTIN BRUNCH SPOT - LATER

The restaurant is very bougie/hipster. "Tame Impala," or
something evocative of them is on. A SERVER, any age,
ethnicity, drops two coffees and the necessary fixings with
Cameron and Laura at their booth.

                    CAMERON
          Thank god.

                    LAURA
          *Laura* is fine. Worship not necessary.

Cameron pours in some cream, takes a drink.

                    CAMERON
          I really can't thank you enough fo--

                    LAURA
          Don't mention it.  Seriously. So,
          were we supposed to meet several
          times? This is all kinda hard to
          believe...

Laura takes out her phone, scrolls a bit, and hands it to
Cameron. It's the photo of Cameron sick outside of Spirit of
'77. Cameron glances, and hands the phone back immediately.

                    CAMERON
          OH NO!
              (beat)
          I for sure didn't follow you. That's
          all I know. You live in Portland or
          here?

                    LAURA
          Portland has always been home.

                    CAMERON
          Same. Love it or nah?

                    LAURA
          Well, being Latina, and the first
          person in my family born in America,
          growing up in Portland hasn't been a
          great cultural experience. Haven't
          even done any super basic stuff like
          Quinceaneras unfortunately...
              (beat)
          I can't get over this. Seriously,
          have you seen "YOU?"

                    CAMERON
          Um, I'm just here until tomorrow.
          Not stalking you. I have texts and
          emails to support this statement.
          Why are you here?

                    LAURA
          I came with some girls to surprise a
          friend for her 40th birthday last
          night.
              (beat)
          You were pretty wasted. This seems
          like a common thing.

                    CAMERON
          That level? Not too common, but too
          common recently. Uncommon enough
          that I documented the occasion.

He brings up the Nick Nolte selfies in his phone and hands
it to her.

                    LAURA
          GUH! Who did the Freddy Krueger make
          up?

Laura hands the phone back.

                    CAMERON
          Jim Beam and Pablo Escobar.

They share a quiet laugh, and the eyes lock. Uh oh...

INT.  AUSTIN BRUNCH SPOT - LATER

Cameron and Laura sit across from one another laughing.
It's dark out now. Same table, same place. A couple of half
full beers in front of them. Cameron is mid story...

                    CAMERON
          So, Peggy shows up at my school, I'm
          in third grade. Were lined up outside
          before class, she rounds the corner
          and grabs the kid, Paul, by the
          collar. Screams "LITTLE RAT BASTARD,"
          and straight slaps him across face.
          A nine year old. I was never bullied
          again, by anyone. Craziest part,
          this kid and his family end up coming
          to our house for dinner, ON MULTIPLE
          OCCASIONS. She invited them. I think
          Peggy and the parents are friends.

                    LAURA
          Let it be known slapping other peoples
          children yields positive results.

They both laugh and take a drink.

                    LAURA (CONT'D)
          Tell me non-violent things about
          her.

                    CAMERON
          She's 85. NO! 86, runs a diner part
          time. She volunteers at an animal
          shelter, and in the fall she tutors
          english. She recently bailed me out
          of jail...
               (beat)
          on her 86th birthday...missing a
          Blazer game I was supposed to take
          her to...for her birthday...

                    LAURA
          Do you have ANY redeeming qualities?

                    CAMERON
          No. Check this out.

Cameron takes the list from his pocket. He unfolds the paper
and puts it on the table top.

                    CAMERON (CONT'D)
          If I finish this list before she
          dies, I inherit a fortune. I don't,
          I get nothing. It's like something
          out of a shitty movie.

Laura reads the list.

                    LAURA
          A 'FORTUNE?!' How much is it?

                    CAMERON
          She won't tell me. Honestly, there's
          nothing in the end for all I know.
          Or it's dirty money in a way...I'm
          basically getting an allowance in
          the mean time.

                    LAURA
          Charmed life. I should do a bucket
          list. Just live some fucking life.
          Take advantage of the post COVID
          world, ya know?

Cameron is speechless. These are Peggy's words.

                    CAMERON
          Come with me.

Laura laughs hard. Cameron stares at her.

                    LAURA
          You're serious?

                    CAMERON
          You're a thirty-six year old divorce
          lawyer on a break from work. You're
          from Portland. Lived there your whole
          life, except college at U of O. You
          want to adventure, contemplate life,
          gain some understanding by expanding
          your world. Your parents died in a
          car accident a few years ago. You've
          earned everything in your life. Your
          friend...Amy?

                    LAURA
          Ashley.


                    CAMERON
          Ashley! She is watching your cat,
          Stanley. Named after Stanley from
          'The Office,' cause she's as grumpy
          as he is. You want to free yourself
          from your boring, shitty EX that
          cheated on you. And the best way to
          get over someone is to fuck, this
          guy.
               (points at self)
          It actually might force you back
          into his arms. It'll be so mediocre
          for you.


                    LAURA
          Way to sell it.


                    CAMERON
          Were Millennial stereotypes that
          play video games, and love music and
          movies from the eighties and nineties.
          We have the same favorite Rocky movie
          for fucks sake!


                    LAURA
          Rocky 4. Cause we enjoy montages...


                    CAMERON
          Cause we enjoy montages!
               (beat)
          What else do you need to know? What
          do I need to know?


                    LAURA
          Sounds fun, minus the mediocre sex.
          But you knowing factoids about me,
          and our mutual love of Rocky 4 doesn't
          have me convinced you won't murder
          me and wear my skin like a cape, so
          I'm sending my location to ALL my
          friends, NOT YOU, and we are following
          each other on ALL social media.


                    CAMERON
          Lay off the true crime podcasts.
          S.S.D.G.M. and all that, sure, but
          yikes.


                    LAURA
          I love "My Favorite Murder."

                    CAMERON
          We all do.
               (beat)
          Come with me. You can cut bait
          anytime.

                    LAURA
          Ha "Cut bait." I'll remember that.
               (beat)
          This, you and me, it can't be a thing.
          I'm still kinda off and on sleeping
          with my ex Sebastian an--

                    CAMERON
          Sebastian?!

He laughs.

                    LAURA
          Come on...Sebastian Stan? Hello.

                    CAMERON
          But also an animated Jamaican crab.

                    LAURA
          Fair point. I didn't see a lot of
          red flags because he's cute, and
          sweet, and dresses like James Bond.
          Craig era Tom Ford James Bond.
          Basically I'm still getting my
          bearings.

                    CAMERON
          Peggy says I look like Daniel Craig.

Laura holds back the laughter.

                    CAMERON (CONT'D)
          I got it. Crystal clear. FYI my quasi-
          girlfriend's boyfriend that I didn't
          know existed walked in on us recently,
          so you're safe on this not being a
          thing.

                    LAURA
          Good. And if you get as shitty as
          you were last night at any point,
          I'm out. Keep **yourself** accountable.
          I'm not your babysitter.

                    CAMERON
          Totally! Sooooo...yes?

                    LAURA
          Fuck it. I already missed my flight
          home anyway. Yolo!

                    CAMERON
          "Yolo?" Really?

                    LAURA
          Hell yeah 'Yolo.'

                    CAMERON
          Wow. Already regretting this.

Cameron raises his eye brows as he glances at the list.

                    CAMERON (CONT'D)
          You up for a real TEXAS activity
          first? I promise it'll be "lit."

INT.  AUSTIN SHOOTING RANGE - LATER

Cameron and Laura adorned with ear/eye protection, are being
escorted by DARRON ENGLISH (Stephen Lang type) the 60
something, 6'5", salt and pepper haired, tan, extremely fit,
range master, to their firing lane.

Darron is very matter of fact. Not a "gun nut/weirdo" by any
means in terms of his attitude. Very serious and straight
forward demeanor.

All of them stop at the end of the line. A handgun, and
ammunition already prepared on the surface in front of them.
We see a target down range. Darron removes his ear protection.
Cameron and Laura do too.

                    DARRON
          I'm told you two are first timers.
          That's great. I'm Darron English,
          the range instructor here. Cutting
          to the chase, most important thing,
          don't let the weapon intimidate you.
          Most handguns can be operated by
          children age six. My daughter was
          able to properly discharge a weapon
          at age 4.

Darron picks up a pistol from a table at the close end of
the range, going through the steps aloud, and demonstrating.

                    DARRON (CONT'D)
          This button here will release the
          magazine. When you need to reload,
          press this button.  Press the mag in
          firmly. DO NOT. I REPEAT.
                         (MORE)

                    DARRON (CONT'D)
          DO NOT LOAD THIS WEAPON SEAGAL STYLE
          IN "OUT FOR JUSTICE." If I see you
          slap a mag into a weapon so help
          me...

Cameron and Laura shake their heads "we won't."

                    DARRON (CONT'D)
          Safety. Red means DEAD. This is a
          coiled fucking viper now. Respect
          it! You respect it?

Cameron and Laura nod.

                    DARRON (CONT'D)
          Excellent. Now, pull the hammer back
          on the weapon. This loads a round
          into the chamber. One round will
          fire for every trigger pull. DO NOT
          REPEATEDLY PULL THE TRIGGER. THIS
          ISN'T "ABOVE THE LAW." You understand?

Cameron and Laura nod.

                    DARRON (CONT'D)
          Look down the sights of the weapon.
          The front sight centered. Put that
          just below where you want to fire.

Darron puts on his ear phones, gets into posture, and fires
a shot at the target downrange. Cameron and Laura both jump.
Especially Cameron.

                    DARRON (CONT'D)
          Respect the viper, Cameron, do not
          fear it! Again, notice how I hold
          the weapon when I fire. DO NOT HOLD
          THE WEAPON SIDEWISE OR BEHIND YOUR
          HEAD OR SOME "HARD TO KILL," STEVEN
          SEAGAL "LAWMAN" BULLSHIT. Got it?!

Cameron and Laura nod yet again.

                    DARRON (CONT'D)
          Excellent. Who's first?

Laura pushes Cameron forward to seemingly volunteer.

                    DARRON (CONT'D)
          Point, aim, exhale, fire.

Cameron picks up the gun.

                    CAMERON
          It's heavy.

                    DARRON
          It's real, so yeah.

Cameron glances at him. He points, aims, fires. He tags the
paper, just missing the target area.

                    CAMERON
          Fuck yeah!

He swings around with the gun in his hand.

                    DARRON
          Crap almighty, boy! Always be looking
          at where the gun is aiming! This
          isn't "Under Siege!!"

Cameron drops the gun on the table.

                    DARRON (CONT'D)
          Am I on America's stupidest idiot
          morons show?! Don't drop it! PLACE
          it. Definitely not a shot worthy of
          a "fuck yeah," either. ALWAYS point
          it that way.  Now go ahead and shoot
          until you empty the mag.

Cameron fires off the rest, hitting the target more often
than not, accuracy is not anything to write home about. He
pops out the mag, and puts the gun on the bench. Laura steps
and does the loading and the pulling and etc.

                    LAURA
          Ok. Point, aim, exhale, fire.

Laura does the thing, and misses the target completely.
Cameron laughs. Darron notices.

                    DARRON
          Aim a little left, and a little
          higher. Breathe.
                 (turns to Cameron)
          And you, I bet you fifty bucks she
          gets a better shot than any of yours.

                    LAURA
          I want in on that.

                    CAMERON
          You're both on.

Laura points, aims, exhales, fires, and gets inside the rings.
Not quite as good as Cameron's best, but close.

Laura fires again. Slightly worse than the last. She fires again, another complete miss.

                    CAMERON (CONT'D)
          Not shaking my confidence here...

Laura takes a breath, exhales, and fires off the rest of the clip, getting SEVERAL shots closer to the center than Cameron. One inside the bullseye.

                    CAMERON (CONT'D)
          Fuck.
               (beat)
          Darron, you have Venmo?

                    DARRON
          A memo? I'm not billing you!

Laura puts the gun down, and gets out her small front pocket wallet, takes out $50, and hands it to Darron.

                    LAURA
          You owe me.

                    DARRON
          Thank ya, miss. You a doctor, lawyer,
          military?

                    LAURA
          Lawyer. Darron, you are astute!
          What did you do before this?
          Military?

                    DARRON
          Twenty-two years in the Navy. Then I
          made the mistake of being a stuntman
          for an action star for a spell before
          buying this place.

                    CAMERON
          Was this actor "On Deadly Ground,"
          at any point? Did the man have
          a..."Glimmer" about him?

Darron looks at Cameron perplexed.

                    CAMERON (CONT'D)
          You were Steven Seagal's stunt double,
          right?

                    DARRON
          Hell no! Danny DeVito.

                    CAMERON
          Pardon?

                    LAURA
          Was he an *action* star?

                    DARRON
          You kidding?! I almost died for that
          cocksucker on "Matilda!"

                    CAMERON
          "Matilda?" Really?
              (beat)
          Also...

Cameron makes hand motions indicating the size difference.
Darron stares at them with a complete stone face.

                    DARRON
          Danny DeVito.

INT. CAMERON'S HOTEL ROOM - LATER

Cameron and Laura lie in bed cuddling close. They are both
breathing heavily.

                    LAURA
          Destroying you at shooting a gun in
          front of that man was so hot.

                    CAMERON
          Did you think about him during?

                    LAURA
          Some of the time. Why; you jealous?

                    CAMERON
          No! Didn't want to be the only one.

They laugh as they catch their breath.

                    LAURA
          Your list said "put it all on black."
          Why?

                    CAMERON
          Seems weirdly baller. James Bond
          shit. Do you think I look like Daniel
          Craig?

                    LAURA
          More Woody Harrelson.

                    CAMERON
          I can dig that.

                    LAURA
          Me too. What do you think about a
          detour before Miami?

AN AIRPLANE OVER A US MAP TRAVELING FROM AUSTIN TO VEGAS

INT. LAS VEGAS CASINO - AFTERNOON - NEXT DAY

Cameron and Laura walk the floor in a sea of slot machines.
Laura leads Cameron to a 4D Ghostbusters video slot machine.

                    LAURA
          I have to play this!

It's very fancy with it's lights and sounds and vibrations.
Laura feeds twenty and soon starts making crazy hand and
body motions at the screen.

                    CAMERON
          You look like a crazy person. What
          are you doing?

                    LAURA
          I *express my body* to do different
          stuff and it unlocks bonuses. It's
          very freeing...

Cameron leans in. The game looks crazy with all of the
animated ghosts and such flying out of the screen as Laura
flings her limbs about.

                    CAMERON
          You're more comfortable *expressing
          your body* than I am. Not for me.

                    LAURA
          Wait! You've gotta see a bonus round!
              (beat)
          Like this! Oh my god!

                    CAMERON
          What's happening?

                    LAURA
          I roast these marshmallows, I win
          money. I'm at One-seventy!

                    CAMERON
          Holy shit. I get this. This is
          amazing! You're over a thousand!

                    LAURA
          Sebastian and I would come to Vegas
          and we always lost! He said _I_ was
          bad luck. HA!

People from the casino floor begin to crowd around as the
machine goes ape shit. Eventually it spits out a voucher
indicating $7833.87. Laura snags it and stuffs it in her
bra. They walk away from the adoring crowd and hug hard.

                    CAMERON
          That was insane! I see why people
          get addicted to gambling...

                    LAURA
          This makes up for every shitty,
          boring, basic Vegas trip with
          Sebastian! Not better than the drunk,
          super fun, blurry ones with my
          friends, but still. This covers my
          rent for MONTHS! Fuck I am HYPED.
          Let's do your thing!

Before he can react, Laura grabs his hand and leads him away.

INT.  LAS VEGAS CASINO - LATER

Cameron and Laura approach the roulette table. Cameron puts
down a fifty dollar chip. The DEALER (any age/ethnicity)
snags the chip and looks at Cameron.

                    DEALER
          What's your bet, sir?

                    CAMERON
          Black.

The dealer places the chip. The marble spins round, and
eventually lands on red.

                    CAMERON (CONT'D)
          And now reality.

They turn and get a few steps before Cameron stops. He looks
to Laura with her eight thousand dollars, then his chips.

                    LAURA
          Don't look at me. I'm **keeping** my
          eight grand, buddy.

They step back to the roulette table. Cameron puts down two-
thousand in chips.

                    CAMERON
          Black thirty-three.

The dealer counts, then looks to the PIT BOSS (any
age/etnicity).

                    DEALER
          Two - thousand on black thirty three.

The Pit boss nods. People places bets. The dealer spins the
wheel. The marble spins around, tapping the silver rails,
and wouldn't you know it, it lands on black 33. Cameron and
Laura freak out with those around them.

                    DEALER (CONT'D)
          Congratulations, sir!

The dealer hands Cameron a tray with his winnings. Cameron
and Laura sneak away, and scuttle off to an empty elevator.

INT.   ELEVATOR IN VEGAS CASINO - CONTINUOUS

Cameron hits the button for their floor and the doors close.
A sad MUZAK version of "Young American," by David Bowie is
playing. They both notice.

                    LAURA
          This is borderline criminal. This is
          my favorite song. FAVORITE SONG.
          Ever. The cover by "The Cure,"
          was...fine. This...this is uncalled
          for.

                    CAMERON
          Are you gonna ask to speak to the
          management?

                    LAURA
          You literally WERE the management.

                    CAMERON
          Woah....you're right. Thank you for
          bringing that to the attention of...
          the management.

They make out furiously.

INT.   VEGAS HOTEL SUITE - LATER

Cameron and Laura sit in robes eating room service. The list
is on the table in front of them. The TV is on in the
background.

                    LAURA
          We gonna blow it all on room service
          and mini bar charges?

                    CAMERON
          Looking into buying the Denver
          Broncos.

                    LAURA
          The Denver Broncos?! UUUGGGHHH You
          just don't understand football,
          Cameron.


                    CAMERON
          You got that reference! Amazing.

                    LAURA
          Simpsons?! All day err day.

An ASPCA commercial with Sarah MacLachlan comes on. Cameron
is mesmerized/saddened by it.

                    LAURA (CONT'D)
          How old is this commercial?
               (beat)
          Are you crying?

He is.

                    CAMERON
          I feel...feelings.

Laura leans over and embraces him.

                    LAURA
          You can feel feelings. That's ok.

                    CAMERON
          I'm giving Sarah MacLachlan money.
          Cats are great, dogs are great.
          Whatever, I'm giving them money.

Cameron picks up his phone and types in the web address.

                    LAURA
          You're dead serious.

                    CAMERON
          I'm on a high right now. Fuck it.

                    LAURA
          Crossing help the animals off.

                    CAMERON
          YES! Also that! Shit.
               (beat)
          There's an Apple Pay button.
               (beat)
          Done.

Laura finds the list and a pen and draws a line through "help
the animals."

                    CAMERON (CONT'D)
          Can we do it? I wanna do it with
          you.

                    LAURA
          Yes, but...*"I must break you"*
               (*bad Russian accent*)

Laura starts kissing him.

                    CAMERON
          Weirdly this is not my first Dolph
          Lundgren related boner.

                    LAURA
          Excuse me?

                    CAMERON
          "Masters of the Universe," was on in
          the background once.

Laura laughs and pounces on him.

INT. VEGAS HOTEL - NIGHT - LATER

It's pitch black in the room. Cameron gets up and walks toward
the bathroom. He's quiet but Laura wakes nonetheless.

                    LAURA
          Come back to bed.

                    CAMERON
          I gotta pee.

                    LAURA
          Just come back to bed.

                    CAMERON
          I'll be quick.

                    LAURA
          Hurry up.

Cameron pees and returns to the bed.

                    LAURA (CONT'D)
          Don't sneak out again.

                    CAMERON
          What? I wasn...

                    LAURA
          Just don't.

She pulls him in close and closes her eyes. Cameron lies
there unsettled.

INT.   VEGAS HOTEL - NEXT MORNING

Laura is mostly dressed and comes over to shake Cameron, who
is still crashed in bed. He grunts.

                    LAURA
          Get up. We have to go soon.

                    CAMERON
          Whyyyyyyyyy?!

He groans and half attempts to turn over. Laura stands staring
at him.

                    LAURA
          I'll get in the shower with you if
          you don't get my hair wet.

He pops up and sprints to the bathroom. Laura smacks his
butt as he goes by, and follows.

EXT.   SPEED VEGAS - DAY

Race track with rare/exotic cars you can race/drive on track
at high speeds

INT.   FERRARI SF90 STRADALE - CONTINUOUS

Cameron sits behind the wheel of a red FERRARI SF90 STRADALE
with his super cool instructor CORTEZ 40s/50s (Antonio
Banderas Type). We can see Laura through the passenger window
waiting for her turn. Everyone is decked out in racing suits
and helmets, Laura holding hers to her hip.

                    CORTEZ
          Remember, accelerate hard into the
          last turn. At the red flag brake for
          ONE Mississippi then gun it. You
          ready?

Cameron nods as a huge, almost Grinch like smirk, shows across
his face. They sit silent for a second.

                    CORTEZ (CONT'D)
          Gotta say you're ready or I can't
          let you go, buddy. Legal stuff.

                    CAMERON
          I am willing to operate this
          MASTERPIECE up to it's absolute limit
          knowing fully it may result in one,
                    (MORE)

                    CAMERON (CONT'D)
          or both of our deaths, and Speed
          Vegas assumes no responsibility. Are
          YOU ready?

                    CORTEZ
          I don't fear death, boy...LET'S GO!

BANG. The Ferrari blasts forward

INT.  FERRARI SF90/ EXT. SPEED VEGAS

Cameron drives a surprisingly speedy and smooth lap with Bob
Seger "Shakedown" playing throughout.

EXT.  SPEED VEGAS TRACK - MOMENTS LATER

The Ferrari comes to a stop. Cameron and Cortez get out.
Cameron pulls of his helmet, and walks to Laura smiling ear
to ear.

                    LAURA
          How was it?!

                    CAMERON
          It's like...I can't describe it.
          I've never felt my heart slam into
          my rib cage like that. Not even on a
          roller coaster. Kinda chubbed up...

                    LAURA
          You're romanticizing.

                    CAMERON
          Say that after.

INT. FERRARI SF90 STRADALE - CONTINUOUS

Cortez sits in the drivers seat. Laura straps her helmet.

                    CORTEZ
          I'll do one lap going easy to remind
          you what we went over in the
          classroom. The second lap I'll push
          the car hard, give you an idea of
          what to do, what the car can do,
          then it's all yours. Sound good?

                    LAURA
          My ex has a Corvette. Gun it.

                    CORTEZ
          No offense, this isn't a Corvette,
          and I'm a professi--

                         LAURA
          LETS GO!

Cortez grins, then turns on the radio. VAN HALEN 'Runnin'
with the Devil,' plays as he engages the LAUNCH CONTROL

                         LAURA (CONT'D)
          WHAT ARE YOU WAITING FOR?! I SAID
          LETS GO!

                         CORTEZ
          Launch control.

                         LAURA
          "Launch control?" That's hilarious.
          Did Ferrari hire an eight year old
          to name that?

                         CORTEZ
          Something like that...

The Stradale TEARS off the line, tires screeching into the
pavement as fragments of rubber burn to cinders in the open
air. The car launches forward like a speeding bullet stained
blood red. Laura begins to shriek...

EXT.  SPEED VEGAS TRACK - CONTINUOUS

The Ferrari charges the first turn angrier than the stallion
on it's insignia. Fire spitting and cracking from the exhaust
pipes.

INT. FERRARI SF90 STRADALE - CONTINUOUS

Cortez laughs, as Laura is full on SCREAMING. The car pulls
through the oval at the third turn when it happens...

                         LAURA
          I'M PEEING! I'M PEEING! I'M PEEING!

EXT.  SPEED VEGAS - LATER.

Cameron and Laura walk to their parked rental car. Laura
wearing Speed Vegas sweats, is carrying a Speed Vegas bag
containing her jeans etc. Cameron is giggling, and soon stops
to laugh HYSTERICALLY.

He embraces her and gives her a kiss still giggling. She
pushes him away.

                         LAURA
          It's not that funny yet.
               (beat)
          How was I supposed to know it was
          that fast?!
                         (MORE)

                    LAURA (CONT'D)
               (beat)
          I didn't pee this morning, and I had
          two coffees!

Cameron laughs even harder.

                    LAURA (CONT'D)
          It's not that funny yet. Stop it.

Once he collects himself...

                    CAMERON
          Speaking of peeing pants, wanna go
          to Miami, see some old ladies?

                    LAURA
          Gross. Yes.

                    CAMERON
          Hey...

                    LAURA
          Seriously no more.

                    CAMERON
          No. Not that. I don't think anyone
          has ever done something like this
          for me. That was incredible.

                    LAURA
          Of course. Gotta knock out that list,
          right?

                    CAMERON
          Right...

AIRPLANE OVER A MAP TRAVELING FROM VEGAS TO MIAMI

EXT.  RUTH, YVONNE, AND LYNNE'S PLACE - NEXT MORNING

As they approach the front door, YVONNE (80s, any ethnicity)
walks out. House slippers, thick rim glasses, bright plaid
shirt. She hugs both of them and makes an "OOOO," sound.

                    YVONNE
          MISTER CAMERON!

                    CAMERON
          I'm gonna have to guess...

                    YVONNE
          Yvonne!
               (looks back and yells)
          Come onnnn; the kids are here!

                    CAMERON
          Yvonne, good to see you again.  This
          is my friend Laura I told you about
          on the phone.

Yvonne takes Laura by the arm and leads her inside.

                    LAURA
          So happy to meet you!

Yvonne hugs her again, then holds her by the shoulders.

                    YVONNE
          OH!!! You are an absolute vision,
          girl! I'm Yvonne. He's a cutie, but
          honey, for pity's sakes...

                    LAURA
          Wow, thank you! And Pity! Thatssss
          what it is. Finally figured it out.

Laura and Yvonne laugh. Laura turns to Cameron and winks.
Ruth and Kaye (80's, any ethnicity) arrive at the entry way
as they walk inside.

INT. RUTH, YVONNE, AND LYNNE'S PLACE - CONTINUOUS

The three ladies crowd around them. Ruth and Lynne are clones
of Yvonne in terms of attire, amount of jewelry, glasses
etc. All three of them cute, old, small town, northwest
grandmas.

                    YVONNE
          Look at how beautiful this girl is!

                    LYNNE
          She really is! I'm, Lynne.

Lynne hugs Laura.

                    RUTH
          You really are. I'm Ruth.

Ruth hugs Laura.

                    CAMERON
          OK. You've all stated the obvious
          fact now. Thanks.

                    LYNNE
          Isn't he a charmer though?!

Lynne hugs him.

                         RUTH
          You'll need that. She's too good for
          you.

Ruth hugs him.

                         CAMERON
          Nice to see you too, Ruth.

INT. RUTH, YVONNE, AND LYNNE'S PLACE LIVING ROOM - MOMENTS
LATER

Cameron, Laura, Ruth, and Yvonne sit on a lavender cloth
couch covered in plastic. The coffee table adorned with cards,
a cribbage board, crocheted coasters, crackers etc. It's
Golden Girls if it were in the early 2000's. Lynne walks to
the adjacent kitchen.

                         CAMERON
          Is that the kitchen back there; should
          we get a kettle goin?

Lynne returns with a bottle of Ketel One and shot glasses.

                         LYNNE
          I've got your *Ketel* right here.

                         CAMERON
          What is happening?

Lynne pours a shot, and slams it, then pours two more, and
hands one to Laura. Lynne slams hers, and so does Laura.

                         YVONNE
          Hey ok! Now were cookin, now were
          cookin! Serve em up, doll babyyyy!

Lynne pours another shot for herself, Ruth snags it from
her.

                         LYNNE
          Hey!

                         RUTH
          Lynne, you'll be dead before you get
          to the car, girl.

Lynne pours another for Laura, who downs it quick.

                         CAMERON
          Sign me up!

                         RUTH
          Nope. You're driving.

Ruth raises her penciled in brows, and downs the shot.

EXT. THE LADIES 1999 MUSTANG CONVERTIBLE - MOMENTS LATER

Cameron chauffeurs as Laura and the ladies mob in Lynne's 1999 Mustang convertible.  Red. (This sequence is an homage to the "In the Air Tonight," sequence from Miami Vice. Avail on YouTube for reference)

MONTAGE CAMERON, LAURA, YVONNE, RUTH, AND LYNNE DOING FUN/CRAZY SHIT AROUND MIAMI.

INT. MALE STRIP CLUB - NIGHT

Cameron, Laura, and the ladies walk in and show ID to a BOUNCER.

INT. - MALE STRIP CLUB - MOMENTS LATER

Cameron sits with Laura at a table as a DANCER MAN (20s any ethnicity) walks by in a G-string. Ruth and Yvonne sit down with them.

                    LAURA
          Where's Lynne?

                    RUTH
          Champagne room.

                    CAMERON
          This a typical day for you gals?

                    YVONNE
          Heavens noooo!

                    RUTH
          Not since the eighties anyway.

                    YVONNE
          Peggy planned this part. We came
          here when she visited four maybe
          five years ago. She loved it!

                    CAMERON
          I'll try and remember to thank her.
          She visit much?

                    RUTH
          Used to come out every couple of
          years, or we'd all meet somewhere.

Ruth digs in her purse and pulls out an enormous floral pattern wallet. She shows them photos of the four women in various places.

                    YVONNE
          She wouldn't let us come to see her
          when we heard.

                    RUTH
          She couldn't fly here in her
          condition, so she sent you as
          punishment.

Laura laughs.

                    LAURA
          I could not love this more.

                    CAMERON
          I'm having a great time, so jokes on
          her.

Lynne arrives, escorted by a MALE STRIPPER (20s/30s any
ethnicity). She sits and the male stripper walks away. Her
hair/clothes are disheveled. Everyone stares at her.

                    LYNNE
          That was just. My stars. The cock on
          him. Lovely.

They all burst into laughter. A KJ drops a binder on their
table.

                    KJ
          Karaoke in ten y'all!

Yvonne snatches the book, and flips through excitedly.

                    LAURA
          You singing something?

                    YVONNE
          He is.

Yvonne gestures to Cameron, and walks to the KJ table. Yvonne
points at Cameron as she gives her selection to the KJ,
dropping a ten in the tip jar. This is when it hits Cameron.

                    CAMERON
          NO! No no no no no!

                    LAURA
          Whats wrong?

                    CAMERON
          Motherfu....

The KJ loudly interrupts on the PA.

                    KJ
          Cameron!!!! We're ready to see how
          you strokeeee!

                    CAMERON
          Fuck...NO!

Yvonne, Ruth, Lynne, and Laura antagonize him a bit.

                    LAURA
          What's happening?

Cameron looks at her with an expression of panic.

"STROKIN" BY CLARENCE CARTER COMES IN STRONG THROUGH THE
SPEAKERS. Cameron takes the mic and stands silently as the
vocals begin.

                    RUTH
          Honey, you better do this and MEAN
          it or Florida isn't coming off that
          list! Let's see it!

Cameron takes a breath, looks at Laura, and it happens. He
thrusts and girates into the open air. He leans IN.

                    CAMERON
          AND I STROKE IT TO THE WEST! AND I
          STROKE IT TO THE WOMAN THAT I LOVE
          THE BEST. I BE STROKIN'!

                    RUTH
              (to Laura)
          He did this for us when he was still
          a baby. Hasn't changed.

Two MALE STRIPPERS come in on either side of Cameron and
start dancing. The tables of ladies cheer as Cameron looks
at Laura and shrugs as he continues the song.

Laura doubles over laughing and carrying on with the ladies.
Everything is in slow motion now as Cameron stares at the
joyful Laura with DUCKWRTH "Nobody Falls," playing in his
head. This is the moment. He's falling for her.

INT.  RUTH, YVONNE, AND LYNNE'S PLACE - LATER - NIGHT

The house is dark and quiet. Cameron and Laura are curled up
on a pull out sofa bed in the living room. Cameron checks
his phone. Laura turns over.

                    LAURA
          What are you doing?

                    CAMERON
          Checking Email. Thought Doug would
          have reached out by now.

He sets the phone down, then cuddles her close.

                    CAMERON (CONT'D)
          Did you like my "Stroke?"

She smiles, and gives him a soft kiss. Laura's phone vibrates.
The canoodling goes for a before the reminder buzz.

                    LAURA
          Hold that thought.

The screen illuminates her face. Cameron sees it's Sebastian.

                    LAURA (CONT'D)
          I'll be right back.

Laura shuffles away in her pajamas, as he adjusts the blankets
awkwardly, and stares at the ceiling.

INT. RUTH, YVONNE, AND LYNNE'S PLACE - MORNING

Yvonne shakes a sleeping Cameron on the pull out. Laura is
still asleep next to him.

                    YVONNE
          Get up and get on comfy clothes. I
          made coffee.
               (soft beat)
          Come on, Mister!

                    CAMERON
          FUUUUUCCCCCCKKKKKK MY LIFEEEEE!

                    LAURA
          SHUT UP, CAM! GO. NOW.

He scowls at Laura, and gets up.

INT.  TAI CHI MIAMI - LATER

Cameron holds Doug's thermos as he and Yvonne walk into the
TAI CHI MIAMI studio. Various people stand around talking,
stretching etc. INSTRUCTOR PETE, male, any ethnicity, 70's,
verrrryyyyy chill stands at the front.

                    INSTRUCTOR PETE
          Welcome all. Welcome back...

Instructor Pete points and smiles at Yvonne. Yvonne smiles
and waves.

                    INSTRUCTOR PETE (CONT'D)
          This is Beginning Tai Chi with
          Instructor Pete.

                    CAMERON
          What the fuc--

                    INSTRUCTOR PETE
          That/s right, I am Instructor Pete.
          Ah. Some new faces here.

Instructor Pete gestures to Cameron.

                    INSTRUCTOR PETE (CONT'D)
          Excellent. OK. Please find an open
          space and stretch quietly until we
          begin.

Yvonne grabs his arm and digs her nails in.

                    YVONNE
          If you embarrass me in front of
          Instructor Pete, so help me...

                    CAMERON
          You're hur--

Cameron sees the blood lust in her eyes, and falls in line.

                    CAMERON (CONT'D)
          OK...

SHORT MONTAGE OF TAI CHI CLASS

INT. RUTH, YVONNE, AND LYNNE'S PLACE - LATER

Cameron and Yvonne walk into the house.

                    YVONNE
          HELLLOOOO!!!

                    RUTH (O.S.)
          We're in the kitchen!

Cameron and Yvonne walk into the kitchen to find Ruth, Lynne
and Laura sitting to breakfast. An impressive spread on the
table.

                    LYNNE
          I thought you might be hungry.

INT. RUTH, YVONNE, AND LYNNE'S PLACE - MOMENTS LATER

The five of them sit at the table sipping from mugs. Everyone
full and happy.

```
                         LAURA
              I love this tea. What is it?

Cameron starts to laugh.

                         CAMERON
              I forgot...I forgot!

He bolts out happily.

                         RUTH
              I forget shit all the time. Odd to
              celebrate it.
                    (beat)
              It's Irish Breakfast, dear.

Cameron bounds back in, and unfolds the list on the table.
He scratches off "Have tea."

                         CAMERON
              This was always the plan wasn't it?

                         LYNNE
              We always drink tea after we rage.

                         RUTH
              Good antioxidants.

Yvonne reaches over and scratches out "martial arts," and
then "leave the country."

                         CAMERON
              Is this a "senior moment?"

Lynne digs two plane tickets out of her robe pocket, and
hands them to Cameron.

                         RUTH
              Skydiving is tomorrow; in Dublin.

Cameron looks at the list. So many scratches already. His
eyes get watery as he looks at these fantastic women that
hardly know him now, but obviously love him. He smiles.

                         CAMERON
              Apparently we're going to Ireland.

Laura looks at him incredulously.

                         LAURA
              We?!

                         CAMERON
              Oh...guess I ju-
```

                    LAURA
          I'm fucking with you. Yes, WE. Thank
          you so much.

Laura gets up and starts a round of hugs.

                    CAMERON
          Thank you.

Cameron begins crying. Laura, Yvonne, and Lynne make an
"awwwww" sound. Ruth looks disgusted.

                    RUTH
          Keep it together.

                    CAMERON
          You're so mean. I see why Peggy likes
          you best.

Cameron pulls the reluctant Ruth into the group hug.

EXT. CAMERON AND LAURA'S PLANE

A Boeing 747 coasting through the atmosphere.

INT. AIRBNB DUBLIN - MORNING

Cameron is stuffing his face with a bagel and coffee as Laura
approaches.

                    LAURA
          You're up early.

                    CAMERON
          Yeah! Pretty wired about skydiving.

He grabs a handful of trail mix and shoves it in his mouth.

                    LAURA
          Did you go to the store?

                    CAMERON
          Yeah, my stomach was upset, so I got
          some bagels, some coffee drinks,
          some nuts. Cheese. Licorice. Irish
          gatorade. These "crisps."

                    LAURA
          Those are chips. Please tell me you
          knew that...

He examines the bag, opens it, and removes a crisp.

                    CAMERON
          I did.
                    (MORE)

                    CAMERON (CONT'D)
          (beat)
     I swear.

                    LAURA
     I'm jumping out of an airplane with
     you...

Cameron eats the chip happily. Laura gets up, and walks out
shaking her head.

INT. SMALL AIRPLANE OVER IRELAND - LATER

A large Irish woman with a brogue, AMY (any age/ethnicity),
stands inside at the rear of the small aircraft with Cameron,
Laura, and a PASSENGER (any age/ethnicity) all geared out.
Amy and the Passenger stand at the open door, then she shoves
them out screaming. A moment, then Amy beckons Laura over.

                    AMY
     C'mon, girly!

Laura steps up, Cameron stands just behind her.

                    AMY (CONT'D)
     After yah jump count tah 10 and pull
     thas cord. Thas one doesn't deploy,
     pull dat one.

Amy points at the rip cords as she says this.

                    AMY (CONT'D)
     GO!

Laura doesn't need to hear it twice. She leaps out of the
plane without a second thought, screaming with joy.

                    CAMERON
     She peed in a Ferrari like two days
     ago.

Cameron and Amy stand there for a moment.

                    AMY
     What are YOU waitin' fer den?!

Cameron takes a step, and hesitates at the threshold.

                    CAMERON
     Just proud.
          (beat)
     I don't think I can d--

                    AMY
     Sweet Mudder Mary.

Amy rolls her eyes, and shoves him out.

EXT.  DUBLIN SKY - CONTINUOUS

Cameron screams, then smiles, then silence as nausea takes over his face. He pukes on himself in midair, and after a few seconds lazily pulls the rip cord. He lands not far from Laura, who jogs over as Cameron hits ground. He sits with his back to her, chute in the wind.

EXT.  - DUBLIN GROUND - CONTINUOUS

                    LAURA
          I could see THE WHOLE WORLD! It
          was...it was like like like...an out
          of body experience!
               (beat)
          Cam, are you ok?

Cameron is covered with his own sick. Laura laughs hysterically and takes out her phone snapping a photo as he groans.

                    LAURA (CONT'D)
          Was there a Garbage Pail Kid named
          "barfbag?" Either way, that's you.

He falls backward, chute sill flailing in the wind.

INT. AIRBNB DUBLIN -- LATER

Cameron is passed out in bed next to Laura. He looks pale/sick. Laura flips channels as a call comes in. SEBASTIAN BLAIR. Laura glances at the sleeping Cameron, and heads to the bathroom.

INT. IRELAND AIRBNB BATHROOM - CONTINUOUS

Laura slides to answer as instructed, and sits on the toilet.

                    LAURA
          Hey.

                    SEBASTIAN  (V.O.)
          Hey. So...where you been?

                    LAURA
          Ireland, actually.

                    SEBASTIAN  (V.O.)
          Ireland?! What are you doing in
          Ireland?!

                    LAURA
          Still with friends.

                    SEBASTIAN  (V.O.)
          When are you coming back?

                    LAURA
          Sebastian...

                    SEBASTIAN  (V.O.)
          Laura! Fuck...
               (beat)
          I honestly don't get it.
               (beat)
          You love me, you hate me.
               (beat)
          You wanna fuck me, I repulse you.
               (beat)
          I fucked up once!

                    LAURA
          Sebastian, you fucked her SEVERAL
          times. And that's not what it's
          about...

                    SEBASTIAN  (V.O.)
          One GIRL though. You know what I
          mean. I miss you, Laura.
               (beat)
          I love you. No one will know me like
          you. Please...tell me you love me
          too.

Laura takes a breath.

                    LAURA
          I love you too...

EXT. AIRBNB DUBLIN - BATHROOM - CONTINUOUS

Cameron is listening just outside the door. He slinks to the
bed.

INT. AIRBNB DUBLIN - NEXT MORNING

Laura is already up as Cameron is stirring.

                    LAURA
          Get up! It's asshole tourist time!

                    CAMERON
          Fuuucckkkkk...IT NEVER ENDS!

MONTAGE/CUTS OF CAMERON AND LAURA IN FAMOUS PLACES IN IRELAND.

NEW DAY - THEY HELP SOME LOACLS GET THEIR CAR OUT OF A DITCH.

EXT. CAMERON BUYS THE LOCALS PINTS AT A BAR. CAMERON ON HIS
PHONE LOOKING AT THE PIANO NOTES TO DAVID BOWIE "YOUNG
AMERICAN." AND TAPPING ON THE BAR COUNTER.

NEW DAY - THEY PLAY SOCCER WITH LOCALS.

EXT. RING OF KERRY - NEW DAY

Cameron and Laura walk along the scenic coastline. They stop
and kiss, stare at the water crashing into the rocks.

                    LAURA
          I want pasta.

Cameron grins and raises his eyebrows.

AIRPLANE MAP SHOWING TRAVEL TO ITALY

INT.  ITALIAN PASTA JOINT - NEXT DAY

Cameron and Laura nosh on some insane looking pasta.

EXT. ITALIAN BEACH - NEXT DAY

Tiny Deaths "Us" plays over

Cameron and Laura are in full dry suits on a deserted beach
with surfboards. The water shimmers like a trillion sapphires.
Cameron kisses her for a moment before Laura grabs her board
and full out sprints to the water. Cameron gathers his feels,
and bolts out after her.

MONTAGE OF FAILING AT SURFING UNTIL BOTH OF THEM HAVE
EVENTUALLY STOOD UP.

INT.  ITALIAN PASTA SEQUEL - NIGHT

More pasta and the grappa. Duh...

INT.  AIRBNB ITALY - LATER - NIGHT

Cameron and Laura lie in bed staring out at the night sky as
the music fades into the background. Laura passes a smoldering
joint to Cameron. He hits it, sits there for a moment, hits
it again, sits for a moment. Cameron hands her the joint.

                    CAMERON
          I can't stop thinking about Peggy...

Laura puts a hand on his chest. He takes a breath.

                    CAMERON (CONT'D)
          She's my whole family. Ya know?
                    (MORE)

                    CAMERON (CONT'D)
          (beat)
     She's gonna die. Any day now, she's
     gonna die...

Cameron stares out into the sky, then into Laura. Laura hits
the joint.

                    CAMERON (CONT'D)
     What'd you do, when you lost your
     parents?

                    LAURA
     Drank. And drank....and drank. Slept
     around. Barely left my house for
     months. And ultimately, I fell into
     a really REALLY bad relationship
     with a lying, cheating, thieving
     douche bag.

                    CAMERON
     Sebastian?

                    LAURA
     Sebastian.
          (beat)
     Boy, did he love dating a lawyer. He
     would introduce me with such snark.
     'This is my fiance Laura. She's a
     partner at Drexler, Porter, and
     Abdelnaby.' Like he bagged his prize.
     I don't know.

                    CAMERON
     You aren't a fan of the job?

                    LAURA
     Really just the divorce piece of it.
     I hated watching relationships fall
     apart, and helping assholes "win," a
     battle over a kid, 2nd dog, or 3rd
     house. I couldn't do it anymore. I
     was so unhappy for so long.

                    CAMERON
     How long has it been since you felt
     happy?

                    LAURA
     I'm happy now.

Cameron smiles and puts his hand on her back. He looks at
her deeply.  Laura looks back equally, before she decides to
shake this off.

                    LAURA (CONT'D)
          What a downer subject though. OK.
          Vibe adjustment: Favorite action
          star between Schwarzennegger,
          Stallone, Van-Damme, and Jackie Chan?

Cameron, a tiny bit stung by this, backs off slightly. He
pretends to consider the question before he answers.

                    CAMERON
          Van-Damme. No doubt.

                    LAURA
          Is he from Belgium or France?

                    CAMERON
          Belgium I think. Why?

Laura hits the joint, hands it to him, and kisses him.

INT. AIRBNB ITALY - LATER - NIGHT

It's pitch black, and Cameron has to pee. He gets up as
quietly as he can. Halfway to the bathroom, Laura wakes.

                    LAURA
          Come back to bed.

                    CAMERON
          What is this?!
              (beat)
          I will piss the bed...I'll do it.

Laura looks at him as he clenches his thighs, and she sits
up.

                    LAURA
          So, Sebastian left in the middle of
          the night to fuck...some girl. I
          didn't know for a long time, and
          then caught him in the act...

Cameron stares into her, and sits down.

                    CAMERON
          Well that's fucking horrible. I'm so
          locked in to yo...What I mean is...I
          would neve...

Cameron is doing the "pee pee" dance as he stutters.

                    LAURA
          Go pee!

                    CAMERON
          I'm gonna pee.

Laura smiles as he shuffles into the bathroom still clenching.

MONTAGE OF PLANE TRAVELING TO BELGIUM, AND PHOTOS OF CAMERON
AND LAURA AT FAMOUS PLACES. THE LAST THING WE SEE IS LAURA
DIVING INTO SOME SWWET DESSERT FOOD ITEM TEETH FIRST.

INT.  HOTEL - BELGIUM - DAY

Cameron and Laura lie in bed watching TV. He's fully dressed.
Laura in a hotel robe turns, and throws up in a waste basket
next to the bed, then crawls to the bathroom.

                    CAMERON
          Can I do anything?

                    LAURA  (O.S.)
               (politely)
          Shut the fuck up and get the fuck
          out. Please?

Laura's phone lights up on the table next to him. It's a
message from Sebastian. The message is visible.

TEXT - When are you done adventuring? (sexy smirk emoji)

Cameron doesn't like this.  He bolts out the door.

EXT.  CENTRAL STATION ANTWERP - LATER

Cameron strolls around Central station taking a few photos.

EXT.  BELGIAN RESTAURANT - LATER

Cameron sits down outside of a restaurant in Antwerp. He
digs into an order of REAL fries. He reacts as if he has
creamed his jeans, and gets some stares.

EXT.  ANTWERP ZOO - LATER

Cameron checks out various exhibits taking a few photos.

EXT. ANTWERP STREETS - NIGHT

A taxi stops in a cute walkable area. Cameron steps out, and
into a little pub.

INT.  BAR BELGIUM - CONTINUOUS

A few people are scattered around inside the most Belgian
bar you've ever seen. The walls, the carpet. It's a notch
below a theme restaurant.

Cameron saddles up at the bar, he checks his email. He
searches "Doug," nothing. Then "Peggy," with the same result.
He is approached by the bartender MATHIS, 50s, a big guy who
speaks English with a Belgian accent.

                    MATHIS
          Welcome weary traveller! A drink for
          you?

                    CAMERON
          Beer, please. Whatever you like is
          good.  It's all good here.
               (beat)
          Obvious tourist, eh?

Mathis shrugs, and smiles. Mathis sets down the beer as PETA
an attractive woman in her 20s, any ethnicity, Euro accent,
sits down next to Cameron. They exchange a glance.

                    MATHIS
          A bit. You liking Antwerp?

                    CAMERON
          Love it! Poked around Central Station
          for a few in the morning. Went to
          the Zoo. Maybe Het Steen tomorrow.
          Any suggestions?

                    MATHIS
          Sounds like you picked all best places
          already, my friend!

Mathis turns his attention to Peta as Cameron takes a drink.

                    MATHIS (CONT'D)
          What would you like, miss?

                    CAMERON
          You should have one of these. Wow.

                    PETA
          One of those, please.

Mathis turns and pours the beer.

                    PETA (CONT'D)
          Sounds like you are getting up to
          quite a lot. Are you alone on this
          great adventure?

                    CAMERON
          Just today. My friend is sick.

INT. HOTEL - BELGIUM - CONTINUOUS

Laura is sprawled out in the bed in her sweats. Something
innocuous is on the TV in the background. She looks at the
Speed Vegas sweats, gripping the logo. She laughs to herself.
Laura thinks for a moment here.

INT. - BAR BELGIUM - CONTINUOUS

Cameron and Peta are still seated at the bar chatting.

                    PETA
          I am a tourist also.

                    CAMERON
          Oh cool. From where?

Mathis sets down her beer, and walks away.

                    PETA
          Prague...Tell me about your sick
          friend. Your girlfriend?

                    CAMERON
          Just a friend.

INT.  HOTEL - BELGIUM - CONTINUOUS

Laura grabs her phone from the pillow next to her. She scrolls
to Sebastian in the contacts.

LAURA TEXT: When need to meet when I get back.

INT. - BAR BELGIUM - CONTINUOUS

Peta turns in and leans in close to Cameron.

                    PETA
          I don't want a cute American flirting
          with me if he has a girlfriend.

                    CAMERON
          Flirting with you? No.
               (beat)
          I'm more about action.

                    PETA
          Really? Prove it.

INT. PETA'S CAR BACKSEAT - MOMENTS LATER

Music plays low as Cameron is in the middle of a rant. Peta
is obviously bored by it.

                         CAMERON
          It's just frustrating, you know?
          The grey area? Are we in a
          relationship, are we not? Will we
          talk when we're back home? I mean, I
          might love her. She's still fucking
          ex though. I'm trying to learn this
          song for her, but that's maybe too
          much.

                         PETA
          THIS is too much. Do you want to
          fuck me, yes or no?

                         CAMERON
          Yes.

                         PETA
          Come on then!

Peta grabs his crotch. They kiss hard. He groans and kisses
down her neck. He stops kissing, and looks at Peta. She's
not Laura, no matter how hard he stares.

                         CAMERON
          I can't.

                         PETA
          Stop it. Come on.

                         CAMERON
          No. I gotta go.

EXT. BAR BELGIUM - CONTINUOUS

Cameron hops out of the car, and turns to see a blob of a
shape, a MYSTERY MAN, who hits him over the head with a
club/stick

BLACK

SFX!! BUUUZZZZZ BUUUZZZZZZ

FADE IN

EXT. BAR BELGIUM - LATER

Cameron wakes up in a woody area. He sees Bar Belgium across
the street. He struggles a bit, but manages to get his phone
out of his pocket. 3:11am. Four missed calls from Laura.
Two messages from Laura. He opens a text window.

LAURA TEXT: 12:11am You ghosting me and starting a new life
here? If so, bold move. Respect it.

LAURA TEXT: 2:22am Cameron answer your phone.

Cameron is fading as another text comes through.

LAURA TEXT: CAM I'M ABOUT TO CALL THE FUCKING VAN-DAMME TIMECOPS WHERE ARE YOU?

He shares his location, and a message.

CAMERON TEXT: call them plz (smiley face emoji)

His head drops to the soil.

INT. HOSPITAL - BELGIUM - DAY

Cameron is awake, and looking pretty terrible in a hospital bed. Laura walks out of the bathroom and sits next to the bed.

                    LAURA
          Hey...You're up...how you feelin'?

                    CAMERON
          I was leaving the bar an-

                    LAURA
          Relax. Doctor says minor concussion.
          It was a club or something. Your
          wallet was gone. Lucky you still had
          your phone. Cameron...I'm so fucking
          happy you're ok.

Laura kisses him. Pulls back and looks at him, tears coming down as she smiles.

                    CAMERON
          Me too...can we get out of here and
          get breakfast?

Laura laughs.

                    LAURA
          Let me ask the doctor.

Laura kisses his head and walks out.

INT. CAFE BELGIUM - DAY

Cameron and Laura quietly eat breakfast for a few moments.

                    LAURA
          I've been thinking about it, and
          maybe we should go home? I know you
          miss Peggy, and after last night...

                    CAMERON
          Nope.

                    LAURA
          "Nope?!" You have a concussion. You
          got robbed!

                    CAMERON
          I don't wanna end this trip on that
          note.

Laura smiles.

                    LAURA
          I like that.
               (beat)
          What's the plan, Galleleo?

                    CAMERON
          You play Street Fighter two on Super
          Nintendo?

                    LAURA
          Random. Um. Yeah. Why?

                    CAMERON
          Who's your favorite character?

                    LAURA
          Dhalsim. Stretchy arm guy. Don't
          wanna hear "that's cheating," either.

A beat.

                    CAMERON
          It kinda is though.

STREET FIGHTER 2 CHARACTER SELECT SCREEN/THEME MUSIC PLAYING
PLANE TRAVELING TO INDIA

PHOTOS OF CAMERON AND LAURA IN INDIA AT VARIOUS LOCATIONS
(TAJ MAHAL) AND WITH ELEPHANTS ETC

EXT.  INDIA DIRT BASKETBALL COURT - MORNING

Cameron and Laura walk by a group of kids playing basketball.
Cameron looks at Laura and jogs toward them. Cameron points,
setting down his backpack.

                    CAMERON
          Can we play?

An INDIAN BOY, 10ish years old passes Cameron the ball, as
Laura walks up. The Indian boy steps forward.

                    INDIAN BOY
          OK, Larry Bird.

                    CAMERON
          Wow. Even in **India** the white guy is
          Larry Bird to a five year old.
          Probably because of that "Last Dance,"
          documentary.

                    INDIAN BOY
          I'm ten, Larry.

                    LAURA
          Who did you expect him to say?

                    CAMERON
          Daniel Craig. I told you.

                    LAURA
          You. Are. DREAMING.

Cameron looks at the kids and points at himself and his patchy
beard.

                    CAMERON
          James Bond.

The kids all laugh, Laura encourages them as Cameron poses.

                    CAMERON (CONT'D)
          Yuk it up ha ha. Fine. Young Larry
          though. French Lick Larry.

                    LAURA
          Everything you just said was so awful.

MONTAGE OF CAMERON AND LAURA SHOOTING HOOPS WITH THE KIDS.

A woman's voice yells out. The kids all start running toward
the voice. The Indian Boy gestures.

                    INDIAN BOY
          Come on!

Cameron and Laura follow the group of kids toward the voice.

EXT.  VILLAGE INDIA - MOMENTS LATER

They arrive at the village a few hundred feet away from the
dirt patch they played basketball on. A modest lunch is
prepared. The adults fix plates for Cameron and Laura.

They sit and eat and laugh as Cameron notices a
hammering/construction noise. He points at his ear then toward
the noise to the Indian Boy.

                    INDIAN BOY (CONT'D)
          Building a new temple. Old Sikh temple
          is gone.

                    CAMERON
          Need help?

MONTAGE OF CAMERON AND LAURA HELPING TO BUILD THE TEMPLE.

EXT.  VILLAGE INDIA - NIGHT

Cameron, Laura, and MAMA (40s female) stand outside of the
Indian Boy's home. They all exchange hugs. The Indian boy
hops off of an older slightly dented sedan parked nearby.

                    INDIAN BOY
          Bye, Laura. Bye, Larry.

                    LAURA
          Bye!

                    CAMERON
               (grinning)
          Later, dude.

The Indian Boy and Mama head inside. Cameron stops at the
car parked outside. Laura stops after a moment.

                    LAURA
          What?

                    CAMERON
          Admiring the view.

                    LAURA
          Creep...

Laura starts back up. Cameron slings his backpack around,
and removes a large wad of cash. He stares at it hard, tosses
into the car, and catches up.

INT.  CAFE IN INDIA - NEXT DAY

Cameron and Laura sit in a cute local cafe sipping tea. A
few people sit around and chat, quietly read, work etc.

An old piano in the corner catches Cameron's eye. He sets
down his tea, and goes and sits at the bench. He hits a few
of the keys. An INDIAN GIRL (20s) yells.

                    INDIAN MAN/WOMAN
          Play Mario Brothers!

Cameron laughs, and plays it. Laura is astonished. He stops,
and starts again.

After a few moments it becomes clear it's "No Sleep Till
Brooklyn," by the Beastie Boys. An INDIAN MAN/WOMAN (70s)
excitedly yells.

                    INDIAN MAN/WOMAN (CONT'D)
          NO. SLEEP. TILL BROOKLYN!

Cameron points at him. He stops, then plays "Young Americans,"
by David Bowie. Laura begins to get emotional.

                    INDIAN MAN/WOMAN (CONT'D)
          Mister David Bowie! "Young Americans!"

Cameron points at him/her and goes back and sits down next
to Laura.

                    INDIAN MAN/WOMAN (CONT'D)
          That's it?

Laura is dumbfounded for a second.

                    LAURA
          When did you learn piano?

                    CAMERON
          Young. Peggy insisted.

                    LAURA
          When did you learn THAT song?

He looks at her deeply, and Laura looks right back not
breaking away this time.

                    CAMERON
          Recently.
               (beat)
          Let's go home.

Laura kisses him passionately, then gives him a once over.
His clothes are shabby, beard is getting rough.

                    LAURA
          One stop first.

INT.  SUBWAY CAR - DAY

Cameron and Laura on an NYC subway car. A CAT LADY stands
next to them with a leashed cat perched on her shoulder.
Cameron sneaks a pet.

INT. FANCY NYC BARBER - DAY

Cameron gets a haircut and straight razor shave from a BARBER
(40s, male, any ethnicity), as Laura reads a magazine in the
background

EXT. FANCY NYC BARBER - MOMENTS LATER

Cameron and Laura walk out of the barber shop. Laura sees Barney's New York across the street, and points

INT.  BARNEY'S NEW YORK - MORNING

Cameron tries a few things on for Laura. He's coming in and out of the dressing room in various outfits.

INT. BARNEY'S NEW YORK - MOMENTS LATER

Cameron and Laura stand at the register with a BARNEY'S ASSOCIATE (any age/ethnicity/gender) ringing them out.

                    CAMERON
          Did I just get "She's All That'd?"

                    LAURA
          Your beard was her glasses.

MONTAGE/EDIT OF CAMERON AND LAURA AT THE WHITNEY MUSEUM LOOKING AT VARIOUS PIECES. NEED ALAN RUCK CAMEO HERE

INT. DEAD RABBIT BAR NEW YORK - LATER - EVENING

Cameron and Laura sip drinks, and canoodle. Cameron has the list in his hand.

                    CAMERON
          I should do the stand up thing while
          were here.

                    LAURA
          Undoubtedly the ballsiest thing you
          have ever said.

                    CAMERON
          Easier to crash and burn HARD the
          first time and make it THE LAST TIME.

                    LAURA
          You should really try. You're not
          beyond help. Go for it back home;
          cut your teeth.

                    CAMERON
          I really don't have to be in a rush
          to finish the list. Only a couple
          things left.

                    LAURA
          Cam, you really should do this.
          Apply some effort.

                    CAMERON
          Effort? I'm not...I don't...

Cameron shrugs as if he is unfamiliar with the word.

                    LAURA
          You're impossible. Still up for a
          hike tomorrow?

                    CAMERON
          Absolutely.

They kiss gently. Cameron's phone buzzes in his pocket. He
removes it.

                    CAMERON (CONT'D)
          It's Peggy.
              (beat)
          Hey, Peggy.  What's up?

Cameron gets up, and walks outside.

EXT. DEAD RABBIT BAR NEW YORK - CONTINUOUS

Cameron stands alone outside with the phone to his ear.

                    PEGGY  (O.S.)
          Hi, hon! How's New York?

                    CAMERON
          It's great. How are you feeling?

                    PEGGY  (O.S.)
          I wanna talk about New York! Whatcha
          doin?!

                    CAMERON
          Laura and I are just getting a couple
          drinks. Tell me what's going
          on...how're you feeling?

                    PEGGY  (O.S.)
          Oh, I'm fine. How's Laura; when do I
          get to meet her?!

                    CAMERON
          Aaahh. I'm not sure. On that
          note...Peggy...I need to know how
          much money it is. I--

                    PEGGY  (O.S.)
          Absolutely not.

                    CAMERON
          Look, I don't know what this power
          trip is that you're on, but I need
          to kno-

                    PEGGY  (O.S.)
          Unless you want to talk about
          something else I'm going back to my
          bridge game.

He can hear her take a drag.

                    CAMERON
          Peggy...STOP SMOKING!
               (Micro beat)
          Did the money come from Doug?!

                    PEGGGY  (O.S.)
          How dare you...HOW. DARE. YOU.

Peggy hangs up. Cameron puts the phone back and takes a
breath. Cameron walks back in.

INT. DEAD RABBIT BAR NEW YORK - MOMENTS LATER

Cameron walks over to Laura. He's visibly upset.

                    CAMERON
          Can we go?

                    LAURA
          Sure. Of course. You ok?

                    CAMERON
          For sure. I wanna go to bed. Fresh
          to hike tomorrow.

He puts a hundred dollar bill on the table and they leave.

EXT.  HIKING TRAIL - DAY

Cameron follows Laura on a steep hiking trail, both of them
appropriately dressed and geared. The sun beats down hard.
Cameron stops for a moment and takes a breath as a couple of
female hikers (20s/30s) pass him in the opposite direction.

Cameron recognizes them, but he's not sure from where or
how. He turns his face forward again, Laura has extended her
lead, now turning a corner. Cameron speeds up, arriving at
the corner, a woman goes by. Again, Cameron is sure he knows
her. He shakes it off, and pushes ahead.

Laura hits the crest of a small hill in the distance. Cameron
jogs for a moment to try and catch her, as Peta from Belgium
passes. Cameron pulls a 180.

All of the women that have passed the other direction, and many joining behind them, are now following him, including Peta.

Cameron's face goes white with fear. He turns, tries to run, but it's as if his legs are made of lead weights. He pushes his legs as hard as he can, but barely moves.

Laura is out of sight. He turns back to face them. He knows who they are now. All exes, staring him down, breathing, advancing. Cameron stares right back until suddenly a hand grasps his shoulder. He turns quickly to see....Michelle.

                              MICHELLE
                    Did you miss me?

Cameron screams, but there is no sound. They overwhelm him.

INT. 5 STAR HOTEL NYC - MORNING

Cameron wakes from the nightmare in a heap of sweat. He sighs with relief and glances at the clock. 4:22am. Laura is asleep next to him. He gets up and shuffles into the bathroom. Laura doesn't move on the other side of the king size bed.

INT.  5 STAR BATHROOM - CONTINUOUS

Cameron snags a phone from the counter for light. After he finds the toilet he looks at the screen. It's Laura's phone, and there's a text.

Sebastian. The text is visible, phone light illuminating Cameron's face.

Text - "Yeah I can pick you up from PDX whenever. You should stay over though. Can't wait to see you, love." A nude pic is with it.

Cameron's legs feel like jelly. He drops the phone, and starts to pee, and steadies himself onto the toilet to sit and finish. After he flushes, the light flicks on, he gets dressed in some of his new stuff in the bathroom, and leaves.

INT. MAGGIE'S DINER - LATER

It's morning in PDX now. Peggy drops a check at a table, and walks to the counter. As she comes around, cane in hand, she wails in pain, grabs at her hip and collapses.

                              ALEXA
                    Peggy!

Alexa runs over. The few restaurant patrons surround as Alexa scrambles to call 911.

EXT. NYC COFFEE SHOP - MOMENTS LATER

Cameron is outside a coffee shop with a large cup in hand.
It's light out now. (SFX Vibrate.) Cameron grabs his phone.
Not a saved number, but shows Portland.

                    CAMERON
          Hello...

INT. 5 STAR HOTEL NYC - LATER

Cameron walks into the hotel room with coffee still in hand.
Laura storms in from the bathroom. Cameron hands her a coffee,
and takes a huge hit from a new weed vape pen. Laura tosses
the coffee into a nearby garbage.

                    LAURA
          Fun hike! Thanks! Nice douche flute.
          Good morning at 11:31 in the fuck AM
          by the way. After Belgium I thou--

                    CAMERON
          I'm going back to Portland.

                    LAURA
          Peggy?

Cameron stares at her blankly. He's ripped.

                    LAURA (CONT'D)
          Let me check first available.

                    CAMERON
          I got you a flight. Tomorrow JFK
          1220. Mine's in a couple hours.

                    LAURA
          What are you talking about?

He shrugs and points to the vape pen.

                    LAURA (CONT'D)
          You can have a pass this time.

Laura walks over to embrace him, he steps back.

                    CAMERON
          There's no more allowance, Laura!
          There is no fucking money!  Best
          case, she stole money from my Dad
          for twenty-five years! So you can go
          bye bye now.

                    LAURA
          Cam-

                    CAMERON
          The first question you asked me, in
          the very beginning, "How much is
          it?"

                    LAURA
          Yeah! That is a weird fucking thing,
          Cam!
               (beat)
          I know you're angry right now, but r--
          you were happiest when you forgot
          that list, and this fucking money
          obsession! Did you get nothing out
          of the last 11 weeks?

                    CAMERON
          Laura, you're a fuckin' *lawyer*. You
          put yourself through college at
          OREGON. I went to Portland State for
          a year. You can do anything you want!
          That money was everything for me.
          What am I now?!

                    LAURA
          I love you, Cameron. With every ounce
          I've got I fucking LOVE YOU. But-

                    CAMERON
          But! HA!

                    LAURA
          Yeah, BUT! But...If this self
          loathing, materialistic, childish
          bullshit is who you are...I won't do
          this.

Cameron is dumbstruck. He hits the vape again. Laura snatches
it from his hand, hits it, snaps it, and tosses it gently
into the same nearby garbage as the coffee.

There's a pause. Cameron fights the urge to walk over and
embrace her. His mood swings again.

                    CAMERON
          I saw the texts and dick pick from
          Sebastian, Laura.

                    LAURA
          I told him yesterday I would be back
          soon and wanted to talk. He offered
          the ride.

                    CAMERON
          A couple apparently.

                    LAURA
          I'm done with him.

                    CAMERON
          You've been talking to him the entire
          trip! I'm not a complete idiot, Laura!

                    LAURA
          Cameron, I'm sorry...

                    CAMERON
          I didn't finish the list cause I've
          been wasting my time with you...

                    LAURA
          FUCK! YOU! You've been enabled all
          the way through this! Even by me
          come to think of it! I went to Vegas
          with you to put it on black. I setup
          the Ferrari. Ruth, Yvonne, and Lynne
          got you on a plane to Ireland for
          someone to shove you out of another
          one! Peggy MADE you meet your Dad.
               (beat)
          If you had any question about what
          white male privilege is, you need
          only look in the fuckin' mirror,
          pal. Grow up a brown girl in Portland
          fucking Oregon that scratched and
          clawed for EVERYTHING in life then
          talk to me!
               (beat)
          Wow. Actually. Thank you for this
          moment of clarity.  I'll, "cut bait,"
          as you once suggested.

Laura walks past him, grabs her bags, and tosses a couple
items in.

                    LAURA (CONT'D)
          I don't care about Sebastian's money,
          or his dick, or frankly even yours,
          Cam.

Laura walks into the bathroom, and comes back with a toiletry
kit, which goes into the bag also.

                    CAMERON
          If Sebasssstian wasn't about the
          money, and status, and all the
          handsome cool rich guy James Bond
          shit then why were you with him?!

                    LAURA
          I was naive! I thought he would, you
          know, like...grow?! Like I mistakenly
          thought you had.
               (beat)
          The money is gone...sure. That sucks.
          YOU don't have to change, Cameron.

Laura walks to the door, bags in hand.

                    LAURA (CONT'D)
          And if you wanna talk to your Dad,
          call him. Grow the fuck up, bro.

She closes the door, and Cameron is again...alone.

INT.  HOSPITAL ROOM - LATE AFTERNOON

Cameron walks in, sets his bag down gently, and sits in a
chair at Peggy's bedside. She is asleep, the standard tubes
and wires attached to her. She begins to stir awake.

                    PEGGY
          Cameron...

Peggy's voice is weak and slow, but she's still sharp-ish
mentally.

                    PEGGY (CONT'D)
          Where'd you come from?

                    CAMERON
          New York.

                    PEGGY
          You were in New York?! When?

                    CAMERON
          Today. We talked last night.

                    PEGGY
          We did? Oooohhhh boy. That's a trip,
          huh?

                    CAMERON
          A trip indeed.
               (beat)
          You want your last meal to be hospital
          "Cream of Wheat," or you wanna blow
          this popsicle stand?

                    PEGGY
          They use milk instead of water, AND
          they put the "Jell-o" in it for me.

                    CAMERON
          Gross.

                    PEGGY
          I knew this would happen. You saw
          the world, and you got a taste for
          it. You can't sit still.
               (beat)
          You're so anxious you didn't stop to
          think that I would be dead before we
          got to the front door. I've never
          been happier, despite several of my
          organs failing right now...I'm so
          happy...I am on "synthetic opiods,"
          they said.
               (beat)
          I'm pretty stoned.

                    CAMERON
          You'd never know from the insane
          rambling there.

                    PEGGY
          Tell me everything.

Cameron smiles at her and thinks.

                    CAMERON
          I drove a Ferrari, I put it all on
          black, We went to Irela-

                    PEGGY
          Tell me about Laura.

                    CAMERON
          Laura...well...There's real-

                    PEGGY
          Wait! We're gonna talk more about
          Laura, and your Dad and everything
          else, but I need you to go to the
          store.

                    CAMERON
          For what?

                    PEGGY
          A cigarette.

He looks at her and begins to speak, then stops himself. He
gives her a kiss on the forehead and leaves.

INT.   CONVENIENCE STORE - MOMENTS LATER

Cameron hands the CASHIER (any age, ethnicity, gender) a
five, and the Cashier slaps a loose cigarette and some matches
on the counter that Cameron jams in his pocket.

INT. HOSPITAL ROOM - LATER

Cameron walks in, and sits next to the bed again. "JEOPARDY!"
Is on the TV.

                    ALEX TREBEK
          Earl, you have control of the board.

                    EARL
          Woodstock for eight hundred, Alex.

                    ALEX TREBEK
          Answer here-

Peggy flips off the TV. Cameron hands Peggy the cigarette
and matches. Peggy shoves the matchbook and loosey into her
pillowcase.

                    PEGGY
          Yes! Excellent! Thank you!

                    CAMERON
          Was that Grandpa? "On Jeopardy!"?

                    PEGGY
          I think so! I couldn't place him.
          Isn't that funny?!

                    CAMERON
          Can we watch it?

                    PEGGY
          The question was "Who is Jimi
          Hendrix?" Watch it another time.
          I'm jazzy for now. How's Doug?

                    CAMERON
          Was real creepy to walk in and see a
          hundred pictures of me, like he's a
          serial killer.

                    PEGGY
          He sent me seven hundred dollars a
          month for you. Every month.

                    CAMERON
          Yep. He told me. We've talked about
          it. I accused you of using it to
          fund this whole scheme of yours.

                    PEGGY
          Not one red cent. You'll see. Soon
          enough...you'll see. Why isn't Laura
          with you?

                    CAMERON
          I guess I will...Laura...well...I
          fucked up.
              (beat)
          I didn't finish the list. I didn't
          swim with sharks or do stand up, a
          few things. I blamed her, then she
          told me she loves me. Standard shit.
              (beat)
          Peggy. I can't face her.

                    PEGGY
          Do you love her too?

                    CAMERON
          Yeah. I do.

                    PEGGY
          Then you better unfuck what you fucked
          up.

Cameron ponders for a moment.

                    CAMERON
          I caught feelings and didn't say
          anything. I had no right to be mad
          about the texts or the photo. She
          couldn't control that. I should have
          trusted her.

                    PEGGY
          Mostly the last thing.

Cameron stares at her for a moment.

                    CAMERON
          Love you, Peggy.

                    PEGGY
          I love you too.

They smile. He hugs and kisses Peggy's cheek softly. Cameron
grins as tears swell.

                    PEGGY (CONT'D)
          Don't come back.

Cameron smiles bigger, kisses her forehead.

                    CAMERON
          No problem.

Cameron leaves.

EXT. HOSPITAL PARKING LOT - LATER

As Cameron exits the hospital Yvonne, Ruth, Lynne, and
Instructor Pete arrive at the entrance.

                    CAMERON
          Holy shit...hi!

He hugs all of them, including Instructor Pete.

                    LYNNE
          How is she?

                    CAMERON
          Lucid-ish.

                    YVONNE
          We're gonna head up there.

Lynne gives Cameron a kiss on the cheek and leads Yvonne,
who hugs him again, and Instructor Pete inside. Ruth hangs
back.

                    RUTH
          Where's Laura?

Cameron's posture shrinks. He gives a cowardly shrug.

                    CAMERON
          I jus...

                    RUTH
          Fix it.

Ruth tap/slaps his cheek.

                    RUTH (CONT'D)
          Fix it...

The group of Ruth, Yvonne, Lynne, and Instructor Pete walk
inside.

EXT.  HOSPITAL PARKING LOT - MOMENTS LATER

Cameron paces back and fourth in the parking lot, phone in
hand. He scrolls to Laura, and puts the phone to his ear.
Straight to voicemail. He hangs up.

INT.  CAMERON'S APARTMENT ENTRY - LATER

Cameron walks in the main lobby door of his 1920s era apartment building from his Lyft, and heads up the stairs.

INT. CAMERON'S APARTMENT - LIVING AREA - CONTINUOUS

Cameron bounds into his IKEA furnished apartment. It's kinda basic/sad, but tidy. He lands hard on the couch. Despite everything, it's good to be home. He checks his phone. Nothing from Laura. He sighs, and goes to the kitchen.

INT. CAMERON'S APARTMENT - KITCHEN - CONTINUOUS

Cameron pulls a bottle of whiskey from a kitchen cabinet with a glass, and slogs back to the couch. He gets through a few glasses quickly then begins to cry. He stares at the bottle. He stares hard then charges it.

He picks it up and hurls it across the apartment, then screams in a painful rage until he passes out.

INT. CAMERON'S APARTMENT - LIVING AREA - MORNING

Cameron wakes up with chapped lips, the sun beating down on him. It's as if we have gone backward in time to when he fell asleep inside the bar. He slowly rises, and shuffles to his slippers at the door

INT. CAMERON'S APARTMENT - LIVING AREA - CONTINUOUS

He opens his mail box in the lobby/entryway. Envelopes and coupons pour out. As they hit the floor he notices one piece in particular under a notice from the Post Office.

It's from Doug.

INT. CAMERON'S APARTMENT - BEDROOM - MOMENTS LATER

Tiny Deaths "Jump" plays over

Cameron sets the letter down, his coffee, and grabs his nearby laptop opening a file folder "letters to write." Inside:

Darron English - Shooting Range - Austin

Ruth, Yvonne, and Kaye - Miami

AMY of fly Dublin Skydiving - Dublin Ireland

Cortez Easley - Speed Vegas

Cameron opens the doc titled 'DOUG' It's blank. He begins to type.

Doug,

I got your letter. Awesome you got a puppy. Thinking about a cat myself. You'll have to send photos. On that note, I know it's taken me forever to get back. Was traveling. I have your email now, so I'll send photos of my adventures. Thanks so much for writing, Dad.

Cameron

He picks up his phone. He scrolls to Laura, hesitates, and calls.

INT.  LAURA'S HOUSE - MOMENTS LATER

Laura, sitting on her couch, glances at her phone. She sees the missed call from Cameron. Laura sits for a second, stopping herself from calling him back as a call from Cameron appears on the screen.

                    LAURA
          Shit!

She sends it to voicemail.

INT. CAMERON'S APARTMENT - CONTINUOUS

Cameron paces around his place as he finally decides to put it all out there. He calls AGAIN. To voicemail again.

                    CAMERON
          Hey, Laura...Um....
               (beat)
          I love you. I don't know where the
          fuck my life is going, but I know I
          want you in it. This can't all be
          random, or maybe it is. I don't care.
          Basically, I finally had this
          realization, that I CAN do everything
          I have done over the last few weeks,
          or will do for the rest of my life,
          I can do all of that alone, but I
          WANT to do all of the things with
          you forever. No expectations. That
          doesn't make sense. Shit. Laura, I
          love you. I know now it was never
          about money or anything superficial.
          It was about potential, and heart,
          and just...I kissed some girl in
          Belgium that night. Shit. I just
          wanna be honest with you. I don't
          know. Things got o...We'll come back
          to that. Ok...We can be fuckin'
          awesome. Individually, together...
                    (MORE)

                    CAMERON (CONT'D)
               (beat)
          Call me. AAAAAAAAA OK BYE.


INT. HOSPITAL ROOM - LATER

Peggy lies in her hospital bed, a tray with cream of wheat
in front of her. Peggy takes a deep breath, and retrieves
the cig and matches from the pillowcase. She lights it and
takes a drag.

Out the window it's a perfect June day in Portland. Peggy
takes another drag, and drops it in the Cream of Wheat.
Peggy grins, and her eyes close...she's gone.

INT. CAMERON'S APARTMENT - MOMENTS LATER

Cameron sits in bed browsing PSU classes. His cell phone
rings. It's the hospital. He takes a breath before he answers.

FADE TO BLACK

FADE IN

EXT.  FUNERAL GARDEN - DAY

Dame D.O.L.L.A. "GOAT Spirit" plays softly under the scene

A full on funeral scene in a cliche drama. Grey. Rain.
Everyone dressed in grey/black with their umbrellas. There
are easily 400 people in attendance. A PRIEST (any ethnicity,
any gender, 50s+) stands next to a large speaker on a stand.

                    PRIEST
          In closing Peggy's Grandson, Cameron
          Thomas, has prepared a few words.

Doug helps Cameron with a small microphone pinned to the
lapel of a smart black suit, and slaps his shoulder. Cameron
steps to the podium.

                    CAMERON
          First and foremost shout to Ruth,
          Yvonne, and Lynne for making it.
          They came from Florida, they hadn't
          left in 20 years. Thank you ladies,
          for memories I will hold so so dearly.
          Including sending me to Ireland so
          an angry woman could shove me out of
          an airplane, and the most cringe
          karaoke performance in history.

We see the three of them in the crowd wearing loud clothing
and laughing.

We see a couple of current and former Blazers players (Damian
Lillard, Kenny Anderson, Terry Porter), Fred Armisen and
Carrie Brownstein, Pink Martini, The Decemberists, Simon Max
Hill in the crowd.

                    CAMERON (CONT'D)
          Peggy and I met for coffee a few
          months ago. She told me she had
          cancer. Stage four. Two types. A
          year left.
               (beat)
          Short year.
               (beat)
          She refused treatment. She said,
          "I'm not worth the price of a bullet,"
          when she gave me the news. I get
          that now. Weirdly beautiful.
               (beat)
          She was so funny.  She gave me a
          four pack of toilet paper, a jar of
          chunky peanut butter, and fifty
          dollars every year for my birthday
          after I moved out.  She said she
          didn't have to worry about me until
          Christmas, four months later, because
          "that's all a single guy really needs
          to survive." Crazy how true that
          felt during lockdown.
               (beat)
          I didn't have everything I wanted,
          but I ALWAYS had more than everything
          I NEEDED. You were my family. You
          were a lot of people's family.  Get
          this; childhood friends that I haven't
          spoken to in years, Peggy sent them
          holiday cards, like VALENTINE'S DAY,
          with *cash* in them. Five, ten bucks,
          but CASH. How fucking cool is that?
          If Peggy was in your life, you had
          LOVE in it. Unrelenting, unafraid,
          unstoppable, unbelievable love.

We see Cameron's former boss Trent toward the back of the
crowd crying, as Portland's famous Uni-Piper rides past behind
him.

                    CAMERON (CONT'D)
               (beat)
          In a fucked up way, I'm happy. I'm
          so happy. I'll miss your big dick
          energy. I love you.

The bagpipe plays in the background as Cameron steps away
from the podium. The Priest steps up to address the crowd.

EXT. - FUNERAL GARDEN - LATER

Cameron approaches the basic silver urn containing Peggy's ashes with a line behind him.  He sets the stack of Transformers: Revenge of the Fallen DVD at the base, winks, and walks away.

EXT. - FUNERAL HOME PARKING LOT - LATER

The rain has stopped as Cameron, Doug, Ruth, Lynne, Yvonne, and Instructor Pete say thanks/bye to attendees in the parking lot. One of them...

                    DAMIAN LILLARD
          Goat spirit, man. No question.

Lillard leaves with Yvonne, Lynne, and Instructor Pete hugging Cameron, and also departing.  Ruth and Doug hang back with Cameron.

                    DOUG
          Big fan, Dame!

                    RUTH
          You call her?

                    CAMERON
          Said 'I love you' in a voicemail...

                    RUTH
          Well...alright then.

Ruth hugs him, then Doug, and walks after the group.

                    DOUG
          Bye, Ruth.
               (beat. To Cameron)
          Peggy...I always felt like I knew
          her. I really wish I had.
               (beat)
          Come visit soon.

                    CAMERON
          I'll make it a point.

                    DOUG
          Good. I gotta catch my flight.

Cameron and Doug hug hard. Doug pulls back and laughs, slapping his shoulders. Cameron cracks a smile.

                    DOUG (CONT'D)
          My boy. Sorry! I'm off!

                    CAMERON
          Bye, Dad.

Doug walks to his car, and drives off. Cameron stands in
silence for a moment.

                    LAURA  (O.S.)
          Good, Champ?

Cameron turns seeing Laura.

                    CAMERON
          How di...?

                    LAURA
          Obits...Hi.

Cameron embraces her, and kisses her hard. They stop, smiles
exchange.

                    LAURA (CONT'D)
          I love you too.
               (beat)
          What happened?

                    CAMERON
          It took me a long time to realize
          that life isn't like an arcade game
          that you keep pumping quarters into.
          It's like Super Nintendo. And I'm
          hitting the reset button.

They kiss yet again, when Cameron gets another tap on the
shoulder.

                    CAMERON (CONT'D)
          Is anyone else gonna pop up out of
          fucking nowhere here?! Geez...Let me
          take that for you.

Susan Krieg is back, dressed in traditional black, except an
enamel U of O pin on her jacket lapel.

                    SUSAN
          Cameron, good to see you again.
          Susan Kreig from Baldwin, Harvin,
          and Lockette.

                    CAMERON
          Right. Hi, Susan. I'm very
          scatterbrained right now. Sorry.
          Thanks for coming. This is my...Laura.
          She's...her name is Laura. We're in
          love.

                    SUSAN
          You're kidding...
               (beat)
          Sure. Hi, Laura. Pleasure to meet
          you.  I know we have an appointment
          the tenth, but I thought we could do
          this now if you have a minute?

                    CAMERON
          Uuuuummm yeah. What's up?

                    SUSAN
          Your grandmother maintained full
          control of your agreement until her
          death, and was able to change it as
          she saw fit. She made some fairly
          last minute revisions.

Susan removes a manilla envelope from under her coat, and
hands it to him.

                    CAMERON
          Classic. Ok. What does that mean?

                    SUSAN
          Peggy changed the contract to you
          inheriting all monies less twenty
          thousand dollars for each item on
          the list that was not completed,
          combined with all remaining monies
          in all other accounts and investments,
          and my 5% fee, your Grandmother was
          a hard negotiator, all other
          processing etc. Leaves you with Four
          hundred eleven thousand six-hundred
          sixty six dollars.

Cameron and Laura are deer in headlights.

                    SUSAN (CONT'D)
          That contains all the necessary
          materials to access the trust.  I
          will be providing legal advice and
          any services you need over the next
          18 months at no charge, and thereafter
          at a discount.
               (beat)
          It also contains all family
          correspondence.

Susan smiles as he begins to tear up AGAIN.

                    CAMERON
          This is some straight up "Meet me
          Halfway" Kenny Loggins Arm Wrestling
          for the custody of my son shit.
          Except my Grandma was nice. Not like
          Robert Loggia.

                    LAURA
          Just say "Over the Top, shit." Or
          even better, none of it at all.

                    CAMERON
          I love you. I need to get my shit
          together a second.
               (beat)
          OK. I want to give ten grand to the
          ASPCA and I wanna get Blazers season
          tickets going for Boys and Girls
          Clubs of Portland. And ahhhh....and
          ahhhhhh...

                    LAURA
          Cameron, this is VERY sexy somehow,
          but slow down.

Cameron grounds.

                    SUSAN
          Is the ASPCA that the one with Sarah
          MacLachlan?

                    CAMERON
          Yes, the ads are VERY effective!
          Oh! And one other thing, we'll get
          to that later.

Cameron shakes the box/envelope, and turns to Laura.

                    CAMERON (CONT'D)
          Can you help me look these over before
          I sign anything? You'll be
          compensated.

                    LAURA
          In that case, yes.

                    SUSAN
          You're a lawyer?

                    LAURA
          I am. U of O 2010.

                    SUSAN
          Me Too! '88! What's your field?

                    LAURA
          I thought so. Love the pin by the
          way.

Laura flashes a pin from inside her jacket.

                    LAURA (CONT'D)
          Right now...looking. Was Divorce but
          hated it.

                    SUSAN
          That's no fun!

Susan gives Laura one of her cards.

                    SUSAN (CONT'D)
          Call me next week, let's chat!

                    LAURA
          Thank you! I don't know what to say...

                    SUSAN
          Of course. That paperwork will be a
          breeze for you. It's very straight
          forward.

                    CAMERON
          Don't steal her for a few weeks
          though. We have a trip planned.

                    LAURA
          We do? We still have to talk about a
          new friend you met on our last trip...

                    CAMERON
          Right...

CUT TO

BLACK

TITLES: TWO WEEKS LATER

CUT TO - INT. DOUG BENNETT'S HOUSE - DAY

Doug's house is filled with moving boxes. The door bell rings,
Doug answers, A FEDEX GUY (30s/40s) sticks a NEXT DAY AIR
ENVELOPE and signature machine into his face. There are "For
Sale by Bank," signs in the yard behind him.

                    FEDEX GUY
          Sign please.

Doug signs.

                    DOUG
          Thanks.

Doug turns and tears in into an inner envelope complete with
the Baldwin, Harvin, and Lockette stationary as Nuggets skulks
around. Yet another envelope has a picture of Cameron and
Laura and a letter clipped to it.

LETTER:

Dad,

We have some time before my classes and Laura's job start,
so were staying here in Ibiza (pic attached) a few more days
before we come to visit. See you soon.

Cam.

Doug opens the last envelope, and removes a cashiers check
for $50,666. Doug is overwhelmed, he screams. When he gets
his shit together, Doug looks at the check again in
astonishment. He screams again.

EXT. BEACH IN IBIZA - CONTINUOUS

Cameron and Laura walk a picturesque beach; it's something
from a postcard. Cameron stops to take in the view. It's the
cliff in Peggy's photo.

                    LAURA
          What?

He smiles, and runs toward it. Laura runs after him.

FADE OUT

DIRE STRAITS - WALK OF LIFE - FADES IN AS FIRST SONG OF
CREDITS

PEGGY'S FUNERAL AFTER PARTY/PHOTOS DURING CREDITS

                    THE END

SECOND SONG IN CREDITS "MEET ME HALFWAY" - KENNY LOGGINS

POST CREDITS SEQUENCE

INT.  CAMERON AND LAURA'S - DAY

A well lit, and happy home in a modern style. Organized, but
eclectic. The gold mail slot on the red front door opens. A
manilla envelope drops onto the floor.  STANLEY the cat meows,
and rubs her face against the package, as a little black
kitten, collar reads 'DAME,' waddles by.

Cameron reaches down and picks Stanley, and the package, up.
Laura walks into the living area and plops on the couch.

>                    LAURA
>          What's that?

>                    CAMERON
>          Package.
>               (beat)
>          From Peggy?!

Cameron tosses it to her. Sure enough, it's Peggy's return
address.

>                    LAURA
>          Oh! I forgot. This was in the will.
>          There's space in the spare room closet
>          for them. How long are you working?

>                    CAMERON
>          Probably until dinner. What do you
>          mean "**them?**"

Cameron stares at Laura, pets Stanley a few times, and sets
her down. Laura hands the package back to him.

>                    LAURA
>          It's safe.

Cameron tears into the package. It's a piece of thick white
card stock paper with beautifully written blue script
lettering scotch taped to a DVD case. "I figured out what to
do with them." Cameron pops the tape free from the packaging.
It's "Transformers: Revenge of the Fallen."

Cameron reacts (Actor reaction)

END